The Raging Migrant

Migrant

A Novel

by

V. R. Koti

Copyright © 2026 V. R. Koti
All rights reserved.
This Placement Press
ISBN 979-8-9957890-0-0

DEDICATION

To the Koti family. And to all those who endure, grow, and cherish wins –
small and big.

CONTENTS

ACKNOWLEDGMENTS

This book was shaped by every story I have read, every conversation that lingered longer than expected, and every person who challenged me to think, feel, and see more clearly. Katon's help with editing made a big difference.

PART 1 - SURVIVAL

CHAPTER 1: ONWARD OR AWAY?

It is a secure world as far as the eye can see. Cosmic systems like the ozone layer, earth's magnetic field, and earth's axis tilt are designed to protect - and may fail under extraordinary circumstances.

But what about family? Parents are protectors until they are not. Siblings are warm companions until they are not. What a family gives is dwarfed by what it takes. They teach you how to run but deal a savage hammer blow to the knees when you are running at top speed. We humans seemed to have figured out the perfect instrument for self-sabotage: family.

I was your typical sound sleeper. Storms, heat, humidity, a marching band -nothing made a difference. I could take two naps during the day after a good night's sleep. The only exception was I would sometimes choose to stay up the night before a test in college. But things have changed recently.

Dad came home drunk almost every day. He tried to hide it initially but not anymore. Mom's patience during those days was not what it used to be. They argued all night. I wondered if they were always that way. I faded in and out of sleep, picking up bits of the arguments. For a long time, I pretended like I heard nothing and hoped that putting on a cheerful face in the mornings would make the issues disappear.

That night, we lost power because of a storm. No ceiling fans droning or traffic outside. The world seemed extra quiet, but the walls seemed to have grown too thin.

"I'm going to kill myself; you will never see my face again."

"KK is still riding high on his graduation, let's not ruin it for him."

"You are the most stubborn woman I know. I wish I had never married you."

"Stop it. KK will hear us."

"See what I will do."

I must have fallen asleep at some point but woke up sweating with my heart pounding as if it was trying to break out of my ribcage. Dad's eyes were red and wide open. He was ready to jump from the first-floor balcony. I didn't think he had it in him. He stared at us for a moment. He jumped and landed on his feet as if he had been practicing it for a long time. Disappointed, he got up and took the stairs. I yelled at him but either he couldn't hear me or didn't care. This time he jumped from a higher level. Before he could hit the ground, I woke up. Realizing it was a bad dream provided no relief. I had no idea what time it was, but it was still dark out.

That's that! This cycle had to end. I was going to stay up the rest of the night to confront dad first thing in the morning. Having fallen asleep again, I woke up when it was bright daylight outside.

Why was the house so silent? I ran outside.

"I'm waiting for your mother to come back and give me a bath, you know. She went out looking for your father," grandma announced from her bed. "Can you help me with the bedpan?"

"When did dad leave?" I inquired as I helped grandma with her bedpan.

"I don't know, sometime in the middle of the night."

"I'm going to make a call to file a missing person report."

"You know your father always comes back. Don't get the police involved."

The doorbell rang.

Aunt Lakshmi stood in the veranda all decked out in her signature silk Saree and jewelry. I couldn't say I had any fond memories of time spent with Aunt Lakshmi and her family. We got along fine with Uncle Mohan and the cousins, but we were always walking on eggshells when interacting with her.

"Can you ask your father to step outside? I need to talk to him."

"Dad's not home. Please come in."

"Where's your mother?" she asked while making herself comfortable.

"Mom is not at home either."

"I was hoping it wouldn't come to this but here we are. I'm not leaving today without collecting what your dad owes me. Principal, interest, everything," Aunt Lakshmi fumed.

I was baffled. I had no idea we owed Aunt Lakshmi.

"How much is it that we owe you?" I inquired politely.

"Get out of my house, before I throw this bedpan at you," grandma yelled.

Aunt Lakshmi walked toward grandma. "Hello mom. Because you've started with threats, let me tell you something." The exchange quickly devolved into expletives and name-calling.

The main door swung open and mom walked in almost carrying a disheveled and half-asleep dad.

"Dad was sleeping on the temple floor," mom sighed.

I hugged both tightly. It was such a relief to see them both after last night's dream. The confrontation part could wait, I told myself.

Dad shuddered as he saw Aunt Lakshmi. "What are you doing here, Lakshmi?"

"I'm here to collect what is rightfully mine. No more missed payments. I need my 12.5 lakhs back today, principal and interest combined!"

My jaw dropped.

"Listen, Lakshmi. I'm not in a position to…" Dad's voice trailed. He seemed too hungover to make his case.

"No more excuses. I'm not leaving here without the money." Aunt Lakshmi made herself comfortable once again on the living room sofa.

"I was just offered a job in Delhi that I am considering, Aunt Lakshmi. I will repay Dad's loan."

"That's great! What will your pay be?"

"Ten thousand rupees a month."

"Well, congratulations, but even if you gave me all your pay every month, can you do the math on how long that would take?" Aunt Lakshmi shot back. "It's not going to work. I need my money today."

"Come back with a document writer and I will sign the house over to you," grandma yelled from inside.

"I will be back this time tomorrow with the writer and the papers," Aunt Lakshmi muttered on her way out.

Dad sat in the corner with his head in his hand while mom emptied the bedpan and pulled the curtain to give grandma a shower.

***

I forgot to introduce myself. I'm Krishna Kant Sharma and this is where it all started. Everyone calls me KK.

Before we go too far, let me tell you a little about myself. I did all right with education, grades went up and down, but I wasn't in the habit of topping the class. I was at the receiving end of bullying pretty much my whole life. I had hoped that college meant end of bullying but hazing in the first year of architecture school was the worst variation of bullying I experienced. I was made to confess my love dozens of times to a girl I had barely met and then warned that I could never develop real feelings for her because she came from a wealthier community. I lost my signature mustache during hazing, and five years later, it was still gone.

"I will do everything in my power to make sure your education and career go nowhere," a female senior yelled with bloodshot eyes. It upset her that when asked how I would celebrate my upcoming birthday, I told her there was nothing special about birthdays, not realizing it was her birthday that very day.

On the day hazing was supposed to end, I was the only one from my class who refused to remove my underwear and wear it over my pants. The guy hazing us said we would sit there all night if I didn't comply. He gave up at sunset.

Given the unrest at home, I had already become good at tuning things out, but the hazing took the tuning out to the next level. As someone freshly out of college and looking to build a career, I have three resolutions for the rest of my life: I will never be bullied again; I will have my own family one day that is functional and built on a foundation of mutual respect; and I will buy back all of mom's jewelry.

Now that I have told you so much about me, maybe I should also confess to a secret goal and a bucket list item - I wanted to get on an airplane once. The shortest and the most inexpensive one-way trip within India. Was that too much to wish for?

***

After the incident with Aunt Lakshmi, I was torn between staying in Star City to help with the family finances and accepting the Delhi job offer with a professor's friend. The pay would be more in Delhi, but after rent and expenses, it would be a wash. I enjoyed helping people, but I didn't feel cut out to be of any help to my own family. Grandma and mom convinced me that getting away from the chaos and dysfunctionality was the best thing to do for now.

"KK, even though chameleons get a bad rap for changing colors, it's their defense mechanism, that is how they survive. You must learn to adapt to new environments and thrive in them. It is a tough world out there," grandma cautioned.

My friend Teja loaned me some cash for deposit on the rent. "Consider it my investment for a high return in the future," he joked as we rode an autorickshaw to the train station. Dad followed us on his Vespa.

"I explain things to your mom in different ways, but she never listens," dad lamented as we were getting settled in the train.

Dad slid my bags under the seats and locked them in place with a steel chain.

"Eat on time. Don't work too hard. Call us once a week," dad said, still trying to make eye contact.

"What happened to that girl you liked in college? Are you following her to Delhi?"

"Really, father? We're not going to see each other for months, and you want to talk about Priya?"

"I can't think of any other reason."

"My move has nothing to do with that. She is still in Star City. Last I heard, she is getting married and moving to Chicago," I clarified. How could I tell him that I'm running away from something, not toward something?

"Do you need any money? Where is Chicago?"

"The United States of America."

As the train started on its 36-hour journey to Delhi, my mind was filled with all kinds of questions.

How would we pull through our hardships?

If I couldn't help my parents, what kind of a son did that make me?

Was Delhi a destination, layover, or something else?

I longed for grandma's bedtime story about Abhimanyu. Prince Abhimanyu from the epic Mahabharata was a valiant and unbeatable warrior dreaded by his enemies.

Abhimanyu was so hard to beat that his enemies had to hatch a wicked scheme to bring him down. He knew how to enter the enemy maze formation called Chakravyuha but did not know how to exit it.

"How did he not have an exit strategy, Grandma?" I would inquire as a child, even though I had heard the story multiple times before.

"Abhimanyu was still in his mommy Subhadra's womb when daddy Arjuna explained how to enter and exit Chakravyuha. Mommy fell asleep halfway through and missed the exit strategy, so Abhimanyu missed it too," grandma explained patiently every time.

"Wasn't Abhimanyu smart enough to figure out the exit?"

"He was. However, he was unfairly attacked by multiple enemy warriors who disarmed him, broke his bow, killed his horses, and shattered his chariot. Abhimanyu did not stand a chance because his opponents cheated and broke all the rules of war."

Others had advice for me too.

Prof. Patel's warning was still clear in my head. "Good architects are a dime a dozen in Delhi. They will get territorial. You have your work cut out for you."

"Why you're not starting your own practice instead of working for someone else is beyond me," Prof. Rao complained.

"Don't work too hard, I hear Punjabi girls are beautiful," preached the administrative assistant unsolicited.

I felt a tap on my foot.

"Tea or coffee?" inquired the hawker. I looked at my wristwatch.

"It's 4 a.m. -are you serious?" I fumed.

"You're reaching Delhi early. The station arrives in less than an hour."

CHAPTER 2: CITIES OF CONTRADICTION

What a bundle of contradictions cities are! Skyscrapers and slums abutting each other. Sellers and buyers endlessly haggling over the right price. Millions of people relying on polluted air and water. Delhi had a bonus feature on top of all these. It had composite climate with hot muggy summers, cold foggy winters, and torrential downpour during the monsoon season.

My office manager connected me to Piyush, an MBA student looking for a roommate, who lived a few blocks from the office. It was a densely packed alleyway onto which row houses opened on either side. Space and light were at a premium. The landlords lived above us and our ground floor space was a living room that led to a multipurpose room that led to a kitchenette and bathroom.

Work hours formally ended at 5:30 p.m., but staff were expected to continue working until dinnertime. Breakfast was parathas (stuffed flatbread) with pickle or yoghurt, lunch and dinner were some combination of tandoori roti (flatbread), daal fry (curried lentils), and sabzi (curried vegetables). While the food was yummy, eating out was certainly a drain on our budgets. Piyush and I decided to get cooking equipment and groceries to start cooking at home.

I remember mom would invite me into the kitchen to explain recipes as she was cooking, but I wouldn't touch it with a ten-foot pole. Piyush said he had some cooking skills and promised to teach me.

"One of these days," we told each other.

On Sundays, Piyush was generally away at the Daryaganj book market. I don't know if churchgoers were as regular as him. I joined Piyush a couple of times. I enjoyed reading, but I wasn't as passionate about it as he was.

To say that the market was a booklover's paradise would be an understatement. When regular businesses closed for the weekend, hawkers covered sprawling stretches of sidewalks and drain covers with books and magazines of all sorts. If you're browsing, you could easily spend a few hours before you picked up one book. Piyush would often talk about how it's unfair that the market happened only once a week.

That Sunday, Piyush wanted me to go with him. On the bus ride to the book market, Piyush wanted to know what my favorite book was. When I told him I didn't care much about reading, he insisted I name one book.

"Fountainhead," I offered.

"The one by Ayn Rand?"

"Yes, that one. Why, have you read it?"

"I did. I hate to burst your bubble but there is no virtue in selfishness," Piyush quipped.

"What makes you say that?"

"What's the fun in not sharing your gift with the rest of the world? And have you ever experienced your heart swell with love for someone? I'm sorry but we need to you find you better books to read," Piyush added.

"I'd like to challenge you on that. Let me explain-," we were halfway through our debate when our stop arrived.

While Piyush disappeared a few times, I could locate some magazines on interior design but not much on architecture itself. I picked up a book on city planning that seemed like a light read.

That day, Piyush seemed particularly contemplative on the bus ride back home; it was hard to tell if he was examining the dirt on the windows, the cityscape outside or had checked out completely.

"You know, we humans have our priorities all wrong. We focus on extraneous things and lose sight of things that really matter," Piyush said quietly.

"Everything OK at college?" I inquired. "At least your head seems to be in the right place with your reading habit."

Piyush pulled a piece of paper out of his pocket, scribbled something, extended it to me and said, "If something happens to me, I want you to call this number and let them know."

"Are you in some kind of trouble? Anything I can do to help?" I probed, warding off judgment.

There was silence.

"You can tell me when you feel ready, there is no rush," I added.

***

A few days later, we went to a neighboring mall and got a small LPG cylinder, a stove, some utensils, and groceries to cook dinner at home for the first time.

I would keep going back to memories of mom's attempts to teach me.

So this was going to be an experiment.

"I will get you a new book by your favorite author if you teach me how to cook," I offered.

"There is no need for that. Not many people can stand me, let alone share an apartment with me. You're doing great already," Piyush replied.

"We can figure out the trades and rewards later, but I have to say you're transitioning quickly from a roommate to a friend," I assured him.

As we made slow progress with vegetable chopping and dough kneading, there was a knock on the door. It sounded like the visitor was in a rush. I washed my hands and rushed to the door.

On opening, the door was pushed in with a loud thud. Heavy set men with bandanas covering their faces except for the eyes barged in, maybe three, maybe more. It all happened so quickly. One of them stood with their back to the closed main door.

Another ran in, toward the kitchen. The third one held my shirt and pinned me against the wall. He put his hand in my pocket as if he was looking for something.

"Give me your cellphone!"

"Don't have one," I whimpered.

"If you even think about helping your roommate, I will cut you to pieces."

The attackers' body odor sullied the air before any real damage happened. Breathing seemed like a big effort. I was too light-headed to see anything clearly. In trying to keep my head down and avoid eye contact, I vomited on my own shirt and pants.

The guy let go of me immediately and kicked me into the corner of the room.

Except for the guy at the entry, all the others were now inside with the doors closed. There were thuds, crashes, and yelling. Piyush could be heard saying, "No, I did not." There were more thuds.

What was the guy guarding the door holding? A knife? A gun? A flashlight?

At this point, it was all silhouettes.

I wondered if my standing still was a betrayal. What could I do if I tried? Wouldn't it be foolish to knowingly walk into a deathtrap? Maybe Piyush would understand when I apologized to him later.

I opened my eyes and the first thing I felt was the stench of my own vomit. It was hard to tell how long I was unconscious. The apartment seemed like a mess and there was no sign of human activity. I ran inside to check on Piyush.

The floor was smeared with bloody shoe prints. There Piyush was, sitting on the floor with his face buried into his folded legs. I slowly lifted his head to check on him. A ghastly mix of tears, saliva, and blood covered his face. His jaw was red and swollen. His chin was split wide open. The inner flesh was visible under skin, resembling an upside-down flower.

"Bastards, how could they do this to you?" I muttered, holding back tears. While water was getting heated on the stove, I grabbed a rag and started cleaning the floor.

I turned on the TV hoping it would give Piyush something distracting to watch. I took a fresh towel, soaked it in hot water and began to clean his face and chin. The blood on his chin was already clotting and required some extra effort.

"Are you OK?" whispered Piyush.

"I will be all right. Let's get you sorted out first."

"Watch the news. Watch some pretty girls on FashionTV. Don't think about anything else. I will be back in a jiffy with a first aid kit," I told Piyush as I handed him the remote and rushed out the door for the closest medical store. It was dark out and my slippers made a flapping sound as I ran to the market at the end of the neighborhood.

"A first aid kit, please! It's urgent," I said to the pharmacist busy arranging the shelves with his back to me.

"Man, what is that stench?" the pharmacist inquired as he turned toward me, making a face.

"We just closed the register. And I just sold my last kit to that lady," he said pointing his finger out the door, "come back tomorrow and do me a favor, get rid of that smell. You will gross out the other customers."

I ran out into the courtyard of the market dimly lit by the sodium vapor lamp. Through the thinning crowd, I looked for the girl who might have the first aid kit. I could barely see a silhouette of two girls holding shopping bags and talking to an autorickshaw driver. I bolted in their direction.

"Excuse me," I said approaching them, still panting, "did you just buy a first aid kit from that medical store?"

"What business is it of yours?" one of them said, as she turned toward me, sliding her hair off her face. Her face was now fully lit by the streetlight.

I could barely feel the slippers under my feet, better yet, I wasn't sure they were even resting on anything. Everything came to a standstill on the outside while I could sense the blood inside my veins gushing to my head, as if in a rush to spring into a fountain. I stood there transfixed, in that uplifting electric buzz unlike anything I had experienced before.

How can one girl be filled with so much elegance and grace?

"Buzz off man, why are you messing with my business?" snapped the autorickshaw driver bringing me back to reality. "Madam, do you want the ride or not?"

"My roommate is badly hurt, and I need a first aid kit right now," I blurted out, extending a bunch of crumpled up bills.

"Miranda, we're cutting it close to the hostel's closing time. We've got to go. Those bills are too crumpled and bloodied, don't take them," the other girl whispered, somewhat aloud.

"Look at the vomit all over him. They must have gotten drunk and picked a fight with someone," the autorickshaw guy muttered.

"You like to party and brawl?" Miranda inquired with a smile.

Her gaze was exacting and her smile was disarming.

"Yes, but today was not-" my voice trailed off.

"I'm not sure why I'm doing this. Here's the first aid kit, meet me right here tomorrow at six o'clock with a brand-new kit and that should make us even."

"Thank you, I will!" I said while turning around to run home. I had to pause and take another good look at Miranda. Our gazes locked briefly before she got into the autorickshaw.

What was happening to me? My friend was in pain and here I was, checking out a random girl in the market instead of focusing on getting something for him. Suddenly, I was more conscious of my heartbeat than I had ever been. Could this be one of those turning points with a clear before and after? As I approached home, I felt like I left a part of me behind.

After I went in, I held the chin on Piyush's skin in one place, applied the ointment and patched it up with a few band aids going in different directions.

"I did what I could until we can go see a doctor tomorrow, just don't sleep on your face for one night," I said, observing Piyush's face with a sense of satisfaction. It seemed shapeless but at least it could be on the mend.

"The day got worse after you left," Piyush said.

"What exactly happened? Did those guys come back?"

"Multiple planes just flew into buildings in New York. That is all they are showing on the TV. They are going to shut down all modes of entry into the country. I might as well shred my passport; America as a future doesn't exist for me anymore."

"Say what?" I said puzzled, turning my head in the direction of the TV.

The sight of people jumping off buildings and skyscrapers collapsing after impact was blood curdling to say the least, even on our 14-inch television screen. We must have fallen asleep soon after we ate the takeout food I got for us. I woke up at 3 a.m. and couldn't go back to sleep. My mind was a tangled knot. There was excitement about meeting Miranda that evening. There was also a dizzying realization that the world was not a cozy place eager to reward the righteous and punish the wrongdoers.

At 8 a.m., we walked into the neighborhood clinic where the doctor was still setting up. He removed the band-aids carefully and took a good look at Piyush's wounds.

"If you cleaned the wound up, you did him a huge favor," the doctor remarked.

"I will be working on him for a while; it will take some stitches and a shot of penicillin to ward off infection. I will send him home with some painkillers."

***

I left work on time to stop by an ATM on the way to the market. Miranda was right there, looking even more stunning than she did the day before, in a sage green salwar kameez. To say that she had an immaculate sense of fashion would be an understatement.

I ran into the pharmacy first, but their stock hadn't arrived yet. I walked toward Miranda, trying to hide a lump in my throat.

"Miranda Chatterjee, you can call me Mira."

Looking into her eyes, I initially missed the extended hand.

"Krishna Kant Sharma, you can call me KK," I said, shaking Mira's hand.

"So, this is how you look when you're not coming from a drunken brawl? Not too shabby," Mira chuckled.

I couldn't remember the last time someone complimented me for my looks.

"You look stunning yourself."

"Oh, you're too kind! I think my twin sister Bianca is the most beautiful girl ever. And she is the most important person in my life. You must have noticed her with me yesterday."

"I can't say that I did, sorry. Did you go against her advice in lending me the first aid kit?"

"Maybe. Not everything has to bear her stamp of approval," Mira laughed with reckless abandon. As she covered her mouth while laughing, I noticed her long and shapely fingernails. They didn't even need a manicure; like with everything else, the elegance was innate.

Mira's laugh had a liberating quality to it. It had a way of making time and place irrelevant.

"So, what was going on yesterday? When are you going to tell me about it?" she inquired.

I told her everything. There was a long pause.

"That's dramatic. It sounds like you're a big helper. Piyush is lucky to have a friend like you," Mira said. Though she was staring into my eyes, it felt like she was seeing my soul very clearly.

"Over the past few months, Piyush has become a great friend. He is rough around the edges but is a very authentic human being. He is very well read. You should see his book collection," I responded.

"Well, then you should ask him if he has come across the names Miranda and Bianca in literature. Tell me what he says when you see me tomorrow, same place at the same time."

Could this really be happening? A girl that makes my heart flutter wants to see me for a third day in a row.

"The medical store does not have your first aid kit in stock yet. I can get it for you from elsewhere or here's a fresh set of bills," I offered.

"We'll figure it out. I know where to find you," Mira chuckled.

Piyush had dinner ready for us by the time I got home.

"Thanks for taking care of dinner, it's delicious," I said, dipping a piece of the flatbread in the lentil curry.

"No, thank you for taking care of me the way you did. The pain medication is making me woozy but I'm able to function."

"Do I need to call the number you gave me, as you instructed?"

"No need. My parents will worry needlessly. I owe you an explanation for what happened."

"I'm all ears."

"When our MBA studies began more than a year ago, Aditi and I became good friends. We naturally grew apart when Aditi met Rakesh, the son of a high-flying attorney with a strong political network. But when they broke up a few months ago, Aditi reconnected and started leaning on me heavily to get over the breakup. I started developing feelings for her but having lost her once, I opted to wait until she fully recovered and felt ready. Rakesh now suspects that I lured Aditi away from him and sent his friends to exact revenge. The funny thing is that the guy who roughed me up isn't even Rakesh, it's one of our mutual friends trying to prove to Rakesh that he is more loyal to him than he is to me. All this will be behind us once I graduate next year and move away. I was hoping to find a job in the US, but now it looks like I will have to settle for my hometown in India or someplace away from Delhi. People like Rakesh are petty and relentless."

"Wow. I knew you were sneaking out to probably meet a girl, but I had no idea there was so much going on. Thanks for sharing. Do you still believe there is no virtue in selfishness?" I said, chewing on the bread.

"100%," Piyush replied. It wasn't surprising.

"Hey, is there significance to the names Miranda and Bianca in the books you have read?" I inquired.

"All right, we're entering Shakespeare territory here. Miranda is the admirable one from The Tempest and Bianca is the jealous one from

Othello. Bianca also appears in one of the other works," Piyush beamed.

"I owe you one for that trivia tip."

"Why do you ask?"

"I met someone."

"We know what we're talking about at dinner tomorrow," Piyush said picking up his empty plate.

On day 3, Miranda was thrilled to learn that Piyush had connected the dots with the names. She said her father was an ardent Shakespeare fan and had lost count of how many times he had read the complete works. She said she was pleasantly surprised to hear that I was working with the office of the architect Nishkam Choudhary. It so happened that Mira studied fashion design in an award-winning campus designed by Nishkam.

On day 5, I was summoned into my boss's office as soon as I walked in.

"We were looking for you yesterday to help with a project, I'm told you leave early these days," Nishkam said, as if he was expecting an explanation.

"But sir, I leave at 5:30 after I put in my 8 hours excluding lunch breaks."

"Around here, we work until things get done. You know I like to get all my details right. Beginning tomorrow, do not leave without checking with me first," Nishkam cautioned, while banging his pumped fist on his desk.

"Not a problem, sir."

Don't get me wrong, I was grateful for a job that helped me put food on the table. But as you already know, Mira's hostel was a stickler about when the gate closed for the night. I could not imagine doing anything different or better except complying with boss's instructions literally. From that day on, I promptly stood outside his office at 5:30 p.m. to seek his permission to leave. Every single day. Come rain or shine. When he was available and noticed me right away, he would tell me it's OK for me to leave. Sometimes he was on the phone, and he would just wave his hand to signal I could leave. Several variations of this played out over the next few weeks.

Then came the day when I found out I did not need to ask for permission to leave anymore. I was standing outside his office at 5:30 and Nishkam loudly proclaimed, "It's a free world, you can do as you please!"

"That was ballsy of you to stand up to Nishkam so openly. We all dream about doing it but piss our pants at the mention of his name," Ashish complimented.

"Believe me, I want to work late but I can't."

Ashish Damle, a colleague, was a man of many talents - flirting with the ladies in the office, jokes that sometimes involved curse words, photography, and fashion design, to name some. His creative design skills were well respected. He was one of the few people Nishkam sought feedback from on design.

"It's obvious you don't mind losing this job. What is your exit strategy?" Ashish inquired over lunch at the food court that day.

"I cannot afford to lose this job, no way!"

"Well, if you ever change your mind, I have an email from a friend who studies at Scottsdale Institute of Technology, and their Masters' program in Environmental Design is looking for students."

"Why haven't you taken his offer up, then?"

"I'm done with higher education."

"America is way out of my league. I'm lucky to be watching Hollywood movies on DVD."

"Hmmm…we will have to work on that then," Ashish noted as we wrapped up lunch.

Piyush's face was healing well. Brushing his teeth still needed some effort. So, we paid a visit to the dentist.

The dentist's office was a windowless room with a chair in the middle. The waiting area was a bench outside. The dentist was a heavy-set man, probably in his 50s, wearing wire rim glasses and playing the roles of the receptionist, administrator, and the dental assistant. When Piyush was done, the dentist asked me if I was interested in a checkup.

"My next appointment is not until an hour later, let me give you a free checkup."

"Come on in," he waved me over. He spent a few minutes doing a visual check and poking in a few corners.

"Do you experience jaw pain or teeth sensitivity?"

"Not much, why?" I asked, wondering where this was going.

"It seems like you grind your teeth in your sleep. No cavities but you're beginning to wear your teeth out."

"I had no idea. Why do you think I'm doing that?"

"It's called bruxism and it is quite common. We don't fully know the reasons. Do you think you are bottling up anger?"

"I'm not sure," I lied through my teeth, no pun intended.

"Here are the options for night guards. The stronger the protection, the pricier they get," the dentist said offering a catalog. "I have some samples if you are interested."

"I will be back to see you in a few months; I can't afford even the cheapest option right now."

"Try meditating before bedtime until you can come see me again. Once the dentin is exposed, it will be too late," he cautioned.

I met Mira exactly thirty days ago. Mira and I had a dinner date planned that day, our first one. Mira said she was leaving town the next day, going back to her mom and dad for a while.

It was one of those in-between-seasons days that day, neither hot nor cold, there was only a small nip in the air. In my excitement, I got to the restaurant a little early. I was about to ask to be seated outdoors when I noticed a parrot astrologer perched on the sidewalk across the street. I knew my future, did the astrologer? I walked over to find out.

The astrologer was an elderly person with a turban and a gray beard, seated on an ornate quilt. To his left was a cage with religious imagery and on his right was stack of about thirty red tarot cards stacked. Upon payment he opened the door of the cage. A parrot ambled out, walked toward the cards and started pulling down the tower with its beak, one card at a time. It picked a random card, handed it to the astrologer, and walked back into the cage. He looked at the imagery on the card and asked to look at my palm.

"Do you have any questions for me?"

"I don't, I'm just curious to see what you have to tell me."

"I see big changes ahead for you. You will do very well in life."

"What about my life partner?"

"Are you seeing someone now?"

"Yes, I am."

"I can tell you there will be significant challenges. Even if it doesn't work out, you will be able to turn life around."

That felt like a drill piercing through my chest. I was about to get up and leave when the astrologer interrupted.

"What are you doing here?"

"Here, as in South Delhi?"

"No, in India. You're supposed to be abroad. I don't see a future for you here."

Now he sounded purely sensational.

"When will it happen?" I feigned interest.

"Settling down abroad is in your destiny. Whenever you try, you will not experience any obstacles."

Fortune telling felt like a waste of time and money, agree? How can something working very well fail and how can something completely unplanned happen? Why would anybody in their right mind want to know their future? That too from a complete stranger? My mother was supposed to marry into a very rich household! Look where she is now, all her jewelry had been pawned by the one man she trusted with her life.

I walked into the restaurant hoping to sit inside, avoiding the view of phony astrologers.

"Are you KK? A lady is already waiting for you inside," the waiter said.

In a corner booth, Bianca was busy browsing the menu. There was no sight of Mira.

"Hey Bianca, is everything all right? Where is Mira? I had no idea you were coming."

"Mira will be here soon, I'm here to keep you company until she arrives. People close to me call me Bina, you're welcome to."

I let out a sigh of relief.

"I'm hungry. Can we order appetizers? I will have to leave when Mira arrives."

Conversation flowed over Samosas and Aloo Tikki.

"You know we come from a very educated family. Mom and dad both have PhDs and teach. In Delhi, Mira and I are getting coaching to get into good universities and earn our master's degrees. What are your plans?"

"I think I'm done with education. I just need to start building a career. I was hoping to get a couple of years with Nishkam under my belt and-" I was still gathering my thoughts when Bina intervened.

"Look, I will be honest with you. We have always wanted two things for Mira. Her man should be highly educated and should be as athletic as her in appearance. I'm not saying you're less educated or out of shape. I'm just saying that Mira and you will make a great pair once you improve on these two things. I want you to think about it."

It felt like someone suddenly pulled the rug out from under my feet. What was the need to attach conditions to a relationship functioning well already? What difference would it make to our happiness if I was more educated or in better shape? I was sure Mira would understand my feelings when she came. We would put all this behind us and move on.

Mira walked in with a smile, disarming as ever. Bina excused herself. We ordered Chole Bhature with a side of chopped onions and pickles.

"So, what did Bina say? I hope it wasn't too upsetting. We are not identical twins, but we share the same soul."

"You knew what she was going to say? I need to be more educated and in a better shape physically for us to formalize our relationship?" I wondered aloud.

"Even if it sounded harsh, I think she means well. Can we somehow make it work?"

"I don't know how yet, but I will do whatever it takes. The only thing I know for certain is that I love you."

Our eyes were locked. The pause seemed to last forever. A tear rolled down Mira's cheek. Mira clutched my hand.

"I love you too."

CHAPTER 3: WHERE TO NOW?

Over time, Mira and I had gotten good at making long distance work. Cellphones had only started a few years ago and subscriptions were a luxury. Luckily, Delhi's streets were littered with phone booths, also called Public Call Offices (PCO) for people without cellphones like me. I called mom and dad using phone booths over the weekends but because of Mira, the visits had gotten more frequent. For the first time, I learned that there was time limit on the duration of long-distance calls. When crowd at the local internet cafe permitted, we sent each other long e-emails.

Piyush and I started brainstorming about how I could get fitter. We cut down on my dinner portion size. Did I mention I was not a morning person? But I started going out for runs in the mornings. Piyush picked up a book on bodyweight exercises for me with illustrations of pushups, squats, lunges, and more. There was not enough time in the evenings to exercise and when I did exercise in the mornings, I was ready for a nap by lunch time.

We also listed a few reputed universities in and around Delhi with post graduate programs that would be well suited for me.

"Are you sure you're not interested in urban design or landscape architecture? You know those specializations would be a good way to improve your pay prospects," Piyush observed.

"I'm fascinated by how people adapt to different environments.

Evaporative cooling works in hot and dry climates, shade and breeze greatly improve comfort in hot and humid climates. Daylight can offset energy needed for electrical lighting. Environmental design only, please!" I responded.

"Folks who can afford air conditioning are getting it these days. Are you sure this program will propel your career to the point where you will recoup your investment and then pay off existing debt?"

"I don't know."

"Maybe you can take a chance and apply to some American universities. What if your tuition gets partly or fully covered by a scholarship or a grant? They need environmental design more than we do. That way, you can buy your mom's jewelry back before it's too late."

As I started wondering if I was that bright or fortunate, I remembered Ashish's suggestion about his friend studying at Scottsdale Institute of Technology. My heart sank as I thought about all the expenses – TOEFL, GRE, international flights.

"Fifty rupees make a dollar, Piyush!"

"Don't forget you will start earning in dollars after graduating."

***

That morning while on a run, I noticed construction workers putting finishing touches on a new storefront signage.

"Greater Kailash Taekwondo
Self-defense and Self-confidence
Courtesy
Integrity
Perseverance
Self-control
Indomitable Spirit"

I was in. Those five tenets were our chants at the beginning of every class when I later signed up. I found the first few classes very demanding physically. I regularly ran out of breath during warm-ups. The forms and patterns we worked on after warming up caused soreness in parts of my body that I didn't know existed.

"Taekwondo is about building a peaceful world and a better self. Don't misuse it. Nothing can save you from stupidity," our instructor stressed.

That Saturday, after I got home from the Taekwondo class and showered, Ashish picked me up for lunch.

"I can't believe you haven't tried mooli parathas before," Ashish remarked. "If you keep losing weight at this rate, you might become invisible soon. Order an extra paratha."

"The grated radish filling is so delicious; I wouldn't mind an extra paratha. Hey, about that master's program you mentioned at Scottsdale Institute of Technology, can you forward your friend's email to me?"

"I sure can. How serious are you about it?"

"Right now, my very life depends on it, but I need to figure out where the money will come from."

"You can use my credit card to register for GRE and TOEFL. I could loan you a little bit of money for the application fee and the flight," Ashish offered.

"I wouldn't want a loan to affect our relationship."

"I hope you don't need it but if you do, you should take it because you're smart. You can pay me back with interest once you find your footing there. I can tell you it makes good business sense for banks to extend loans to international students. Also, keep in mind that Nishkam's letter of recommendation holds a lot of weight with American universities."

"Getting a student loan from a bank and getting a letter of recommendation from Nishkam, I have my job cut out, don't I?"

"Nothing worth doing is easy said somebody wise," Ashish quipped.

***

I thought I was done taking tests for good, but TOEFL and GRE were staring me in the face. GRE especially required burning some midnight oil on my part. The Scottsdale Institute of Technology application packet arrived promptly in two weeks. My father got busy with getting official transcripts of my marksheets from my alma mater in Star City. I started researching how to write a compelling statement of purpose.

After discussing the details of a folding door to fit a narrow passageway in an apartment building, I brought up the need for a letter of recommendation with Nishkam.

"You're thinking of leaving us already? I can't hand the finished letter of recommendation to you. Get me a stamped envelope with the right address and I will mail it directly," Nishkam said.

Toward the end of the day, as we huddled around a set of drawings with tea, the office assistant announced, "there is a girl here for KK."

Through the glass partitions, I could see Mira in a collared orange shirt waving at me. My heart skipped a beat. I ran to her, walked her out forcibly and gave her a tight hug.

"What a pleasant surprise! What're you doing here?"

"I had to come see you, besides touring local colleges and applying that is. Bina and I are going to Sarojini Nagar market for shopping. Do you want to join us?" Mira asked.

We hopped onto an autorickshaw and got there soon after. The market was a bustling outdoor shopping center lined with clothing stalls, household goods, eateries, you name it. Some stores were mere stalls with awnings or umbrellas, and some were straight under the sun. The vibrant colors and textures were equal parts fascinating and distracting.

"You never pay the full price. Haggling is the name of the game here," Bina instructed, as we strolled the paved walkways with stores on either side. We stopped at a stall that had a big hand painted sign with red letters on a yellow background that said, "Manpreet Apparel."

"I really like that skirt with the rose bud pattern. And I want to get that teal hoodie for you," Mira said excitedly.

Someone suddenly bumped into Mira. "Sorry," said a voice and a guy wearing a black t-shirt and khaki pants disappeared into the crowd before we understood what was happening.

Mira seemed shaken with tears welling up in her eyes. "I think that guy grazed me deliberately." She started sobbing as Bina gave her a tight hug.

"I'm sorry that happened to you sister. We should look around to see if there is a cop somewhere or go to the nearest police station."

"I'm torn between staying here with you and running to find that guy," I muttered in what seemed like a strange combination of anger and daze.

"I'm sure he is long gone. Let's get some golgappas and leave on a more cheerful note," Mira suggested.

After we placed the order, the vendor put one banana leaf cup each in our hands and started placing filled golgappas into the cups, one at a time. I was into my third or fourth serving when I caught something with the corner of my eye and instinctively swiveled to place my left hand on the shoulder of a guy turning around to walk away from us.

"It was you earlier, wasn't it?" I yelled at the guy now with his back pointed at us, wearing the same black and khaki colors. It appeared I caught him before he got to Mira again. He raised a sharp metallic object with his right hand and brought it down on my face.

"High block," I whispered and shielded my face with a raised left hand with and a pumped fist. As his hand and my hand formed a cross, the jagged knife's tip stopped inches from my face. As he withdrew the knife and forced it into my chest this time, I shifted and used the middle block maneuver to shield myself again. I then let the knife and his palm pass through the gap between my other bicep and chest and clutched his wrist tightly with my armpit. He struggled to pull his arm out, but I did not let go. The crowd had gotten hold of him by that point and he was struggling. And when I did let go, the knife scraped my inner bicep on its way out. I felt my shirt become warm as blood spread to my chest and lower arm.

Mira snapped out of disbelief and wrapped her scarf around my bicep.

"Why did you have to engage?" she asked as we walked toward the medical store across the street to get the wound dressed.

"I wasn't going to let him touch you again, no way."

"And I can't bear the idea of something happening to you. You must leave somethings to the police and the justice system," Mira chided.

"I'm doing first aid for now, I will give you a tetanus shot next, but you might need to visit a doctor for stitches," the pharmacist said.

"Thanks for your help," I said shaking his hand when he was done.

****

The time had come to finally mail my paper application package to Scottsdale Institute of Technology in Arizona, USA. My dad had mailed me the academic transcripts and two letters of recommendation from my professors. I added the rest of the documents and handed the package to the courier guy who delivered mail to the office that afternoon.

"Congratulations, it is a big deal. So, you're going to be a neighbor," Charlotte said.

OK, I should have mentioned Charlotte Dubois sooner. She was an exchange student from Canada taking some courses locally and interning at Nishkam's place for a few weeks. If it wasn't for the fairer complexion and the French accent when she spoke English, her petiteness and brunette hair would make her fit in well in India. We all envied her fearless but respectful navigation of workplace despite being a student, addressing everyone using their first names and not hesitating to introduce herself promptly where needed.

At the end of the workday, Ashish stopped by on the way out and paused in between Charlotte and me.

"Charlotte, how much of Delhi have you seen?" Ashish asked. "KK can show you around on his Vespa, can't you, KK?"

"I know they are showing the new Tim Burton movie at the PVR in Vasant Vihar, I'm game if KK is!" Charlotte responded, before I realized what was going on.

"Don't forget to the get chai in earthen cups at the market, it's to die for," Ashish muttered on his way out.

Charlotte and I were at a red light on the way to Vasant Vihar when the Vespa's engine sputtered and shut down. "I got it recently and it's not used to a pillion rider yet, let alone a visitor from overseas," I explained. Luckily one good kick and it got back to life, so we were on our way again after a few frustrated vehicles bypassed us.

We had enough time to get chai and samosa before the show began.

"How much do you know about the country you intend to study in?" Charlotte asked.

"Does my watching Hollywood movies count?"

"That's funny but really how much do you know?"

"Not much actually. I intend to work for a couple of years after graduation and come back. It's not like I'm going to stay there forever."

"Let me tell you that the west is not what it seems from here. The weather can get very cold as you move north. Sometimes, you will not see a pedestrian or a bus for miles. More people own guns than they do bicycles. Don't even get me started about politics and the state of healthcare."

"Do you think my going there is a mistake?" I asked, scratching my head.

"I'm not saying that. Whatever your reasons, learn a little about the place you're going to. What if you decide to settle down there and raise a family? I will give you a quiz on US history before I leave."

"Ok mom, I will try to read up," I retorted.

"Now about your relationship, I saw how you looked at Mira the other day," Charlotte prodded.

Oh boy. I was longing for the movie now.

"What about it?"

"Well, I know you guys are long distance sometimes but your being in America is going to take that to a completely different level, don't you think?"

"Yes, but I think we're strong enough to weather the separation," I muttered.

"Well, I sure hope so, but what if you meet someone else while you're away?"

"Not going to happen."

"Both of you will still be growing while you're away from each other. I just hope you don't end up growing in different directions," Charlotte said, sipping her chai.

I peeked at my watch hoping it was time for the movie, but time seemed to be moving very slowly. Mira was everything to me. And everything I was doing was to get closer to her. I hadn't felt this restless in a long time.

"Why do you like Tim Burton's movies?" I tried to change the topic.

"You're about to find out."

Planet of the Apes turned out to be a great movie. But my heart had been racing, and I could barely focus on the movie. I thanked Charlotte for the evening as I dropped her off with her landlady and waved goodbye.

"How did the movie date go?" Piyush asked.

"It was all right. And it wasn't a date."

"Just all right? Not many of us have been to a movie with a white girl."

"How are you and Aditi doing now?" I asked Piyush.

"Where did that come from?"

"I don't know. I'm suddenly questioning everything. Maybe this US thing is not for me. Tell me about you, please!"

"Aditi is not talking to me. I don't think she is seeing Rakesh, but it seems like she is protecting me. I don't know if we have a future together, but we definitely don't have a present. Girls are smarter than us and they have a way of not showing their cards."

"What about your US plans? I know you feel passionately about working there," I quizzed.

"I hear visa denials are on the rise after the attack on the World Trade Center. I'm going to wait and watch."

"OK, I have a question for you now," Piyush said with a hushed tone.

"Shoot."

"The girl you pursued during college, what did you learn from it?"

There was a long pause.

"Why are you asking?"

"Just curious."

"I may need a stiff drink or two to get into that," I demurred, knowing I had never touched alcohol before.

"You're in luck. It's the weekend and I know just the place that makes a killer old-fashioned," Piyush's eyes lit up like Christmas lights.

The setting of 'A Deeper Dive' was nothing like that of a bar from the movies. The yellow incandescent lighting was dimmed by the billowing cigarette smoke. There was a 'L' shaped bar counter, and some loosely laid out tables for groups of four. It was the first time I laid eyes on a pool table.

The waitress quickly got us a bowl of roasted peanuts.

"Two handsome guys on a prowl. What can I get you both?"

"My friend and I will have an old-fashioned made with rye, please," Piyush instructed.

Piyush pulled out a pack of Davidoff cigarettes from his jacket pocket.

"Want to try one while we wait for the drinks?"

"No, thank you."

"As a matter of principle, I don't offer someone their first cigarette, but I insist," Piyush pressed.

I almost coughed my lungs out after the first puff. After the second drag, I could feel electricity buzzing through my veins and heard a clang from the spoon hitting the tabletop. I didn't realize it had slipped from between my fingers.

"You lightweight! It happens to everyone," Piyush laughed hysterically as if he was going to choke. "Everyone who continues to smoke is pursuing that exact feeling."

When the old-fashioned arrived, Piyush passionately explained how bourbon wasn't bad, but rye was even better, and how it was important to smoke the orange peel.

"They don't use Maraschino cherries here, but they take the experience to the next level," Piyush remarked poking the cherry with a toothpick.

We were sipping our second drink when the waitress came back to check on us.

"Can I get you guys anything else? Some food maybe?"

"Where is the washroom?" I inquired.

"The red doors at the end of that hallway," she pointed.

"I will order food, you go do your thing," Piyush offered.

When I emptied the glass and stood up, I felt like I was being electrocuted with non-lethal voltage. Getting past the table was going to be a challenge. The washroom felt miles away.

"Will you tell me about your college friend now?" Piyush prodded when I returned. "The food is coming soon, I ordered mooli paratha for you. And here, I got you a glass of water to go with your next drink."

"I think Mira is helping put things in the rear-view mirror. It is a long story that cannot be made short."

"The night is young and I'm not asking for the CliffsNotes version either," Piyush insisted.

"Here it goes. During hazing, all boys were asked to name their favorite girl, and all girls were asked to name their favorite boy. As I looked across all the girls in our class-"

There was a large crowd gathered in the front yard and on the porch. We had decided to bury my father's body in the yard, which we did. It had rained so heavily overnight that some of the soil had eroded and parts of his face and body were resurfaced. We would have to exhume the body and bury him in a deeper hole.

The thud woke me up. I was drenched in sweat, my head and my heart were pounding in unison like a drum.

Things seemed hazy but what became clear was that I had fallen from my bed. I had no idea what day or time it was.

"Bad dreams? That was your fifth fall. I'm glad you woke up because

I wasn't going to put you back on your bed this time." I could barely hear Piyush speaking over what felt like a cleaved head and a loud ringing in my ears. "There are two aspirins and a glass of water on your nightstand."

I stumbled to the bathroom and did not recognize what I saw in the mirror. A bruised forehead and a black eye.

"What exactly happened last night?" I yelled at Piyush, almost in tears.

I ran to the front door, and the Vespa was not parked outside.

"Your Vespa is still at the bar. I'm sorry I got you so drunk. What is the last thing you remember?

"We were in the bar, maybe our food arrived-"

"Nothing after that?"

"It's all hazy, wait, did you spoon-feed me dinner or am I imagining it?"

"You're not imagining it. I tried consoling you, but you kept crying saying you didn't want it."

"Can you please start from the beginning?" I implored.

"Well, shortly after you started explaining how things started with Priya in college, you digressed and talked about your father, the upbringing you needed but didn't get, and your mom's stepping up to fill the void. You didn't eat a bite. I got our dinner packed and put us in an autorickshaw, but we had to stop halfway because you had to throw up. After we got home, I tried feeding you, but you resisted. And then you wouldn't stay on the bed and kept falling," Piyush explained.

As I searched the closet for the first aid kit, my mind was racing with questions.

How would I show my face to the world outside?

What was I going to tell folks at work tomorrow?

What if Mira found out about it?

"I can hear your inner monologue. Nothing a little foundation can't cover up. Take an autorickshaw from the street corner to work for a few days. Tell them you had an accident and the Vespa is at the repair shop. Even better, blame it on a Taekwondo sparring session gone wrong. This is Delhi. People will understand," Piyush assured.

"The aspirin isn't kicking in yet. Do you have one of those cigarettes?"

***

Weeks turned into months. As Delhi's cold and foggy winter began to let up, a light windbreaker did the trick during Vespa rides. A new year also meant a light bump in the salary and increase in the rent.

It was Charlotte's last day of internship before she flew away to the forever chilly regions of Canada. The office manager brought coffee and muffins as all of us huddled in the main conference room.

"You can't get very far with a Vespa in America. You must start learning how to drive a car if you're going to explore the landscapes there," Charlotte said. "If you end up in Arizona, you must visit the Grand Canyon," Charlotte said, "and make sure you have your passport handy if you wander off into Mexico. They will not let you back in otherwise."

"I hear Niagara Falls are a sight to behold. Have you ever been there?" Ashish chimed in.

"Multiple times. The view from the Canadian side is even better. You all should come visit sometime," replied Charlotte.

Nishkam stopped by briefly. He asked Charlotte if she was going to miss Indian coffee.

"I like the chicory flavor, but I prefer my coffee black," Charlotte noted.

"Bring me some your favorite coffee when you visit next," Nishkam muttered on his way out.

As I pulled up at my apartment that evening, my landlord yelled from the upstairs balcony, "come over and have some chai and samosa!"

When I walked into their living room, I noticed how the touch of a woman and a family can make a similar apartment look so homely.

"I just had a muffin and a coffee, so I'm full sir," I said.

"But you're too thin. At your age, I would eat five parathas and still feel hungry," he said, pushing the chai and the samosa closer to me. "And call me bhaiya from now on, no need for sir or anything formal."

"These arrived in the mail over the last few days," he said as he pulled a few envelopes from under the coffee table and handed them to me.

There was something from the bank, a card from Mira, and the sender's name on the final envelope read "Scottsdale Institute of Technology." My heart skipped a beat. In that moment, I chose to ignore the fact that the envelopes were already opened.

"Thanks, bhaiya," I said as I got up to leave.

"You know our son will be ready for college in a few years. He will need your advice. Always know that you have a family in Delhi," he said in a bear hug that lasted a bit longer than it should have.

Tears gushed out in an unstoppable torrent as I started reading the letter.

Subject: Admission to Master of Science in Environmental Design Program – Fall 2002

Dear Mr. Sharma,

It is with great pleasure that we inform you of your acceptance into the Master of Science in Environmental Design program at Scottsdale Institute of Technology for the Fall 2002 term. After a thorough review of your application, academic credentials, and portfolio, the Admissions Committee was impressed by your outstanding achievements and potential for contributing to the field of environmental design.

In recognition of your exceptional qualifications, we are pleased to offer you substantial tuition support in the form of a research assistantship in my environmental lab. This support will cover 50% of your tuition fees. A stipend for living expenses may be considered based on your performance in the position. Details regarding the terms and conditions of this support will be provided in your enrollment package.

At Scottsdale Institute of Technology, we are committed to fostering a diverse and innovative learning environment. Our Environmental

Design program emphasizes sustainable design principles, interdisciplinary collaboration, and cutting-edge research, all of which align with your academic and professional aspirations as outlined in your application. We are confident that this program will provide you with the tools and opportunities necessary to achieve your goals and make meaningful contributions to the global community.

To confirm your enrollment and secure your place in the program, please complete the attached acceptance form and submit the requested non-refundable deposit by March 15. Additional details regarding visa procedures, housing options, and orientation activities will follow shortly after confirmation of your acceptance.

Congratulations once again. Should you have any questions or require further assistance, please do not hesitate to contact our Office of Graduate Admissions. We are here to support you throughout this transition and look forward to welcoming you to our campus.

Warm regards,
Prof. Paul Cook
Director of Graduate Admissions
School of Environmental Design
Scottsdale Institute of Technology

I rushed to the closest phone booth to call Mira first.

"Congratulations but now I'm worried that you will be gone for too long! What if you get used to being away from me? What if you meet someone there?"

"I'd give up all of this for you in a heartbeat. Can we still be together?"

"Don't be silly. I think time will pass quickly because I will be in a graduate program too. We can visit each other until we can be together for good. Once Bina is fully convinced about you and me, she will help convince my dad and mom. Have you figured out how you will pay the fee?"

"No," I mumbled.

"Prepare well for the visa interview. A cousin of mine is still at it after three denials. I'm praying for your experience to be smoother."

"Will do."

"Do me a favor," Mira said before hanging up, "please stop grinding those pearly whites in your sleep, I need them intact for when our happily ever after begins."

As I walked home from the phone booth, my palms were unusually sweaty. What exactly was I getting into? What was I giving up and what was the return? Why was I running away from Mira to get close to her? Why was I letting Mira's sister dictate the terms of our relationship? Why was Mira so reliant on Bina convincing her parents? What if Mira's parents didn't approve of our relationship after all? How would I raise the money for flight tickets, let alone pay for the tuition and living expenses?

When I got home, the door was ajar. Piyush had company.

"My parents decided to pay me a surprise visit," Piyush was beaming with the admissions letter in his hand by the time.

"You did it! Now there is no looking back!" he yelled holding me in a tight hug.

"Mom and dad, meet KK. KK, meet mom and dad."

"Nice to meet you guys," I said, forcing a smile.

"Can you keep them company while I whip up something in the kitchen for us?" Piyush said, as he dashed into the kitchen before I could say anything.

"Sure," I responded wiping my sweaty palms with the lining of my pant pockets.

"Are you excited about going to America?" Piyush's mom inquired with a beaming smile.

"I think so, there are a lot of details to be figured out, but yes."

"Piyush has told us all about you. We already like you because Piyush likes you so much. Piyush's father is an engineer at the Bhilai steel plant and we're blessed financially. If your visa is approved, we can extend you a loan to cover some of your expenses."

"Kaveri, listen-" Piyush's father tried to interject.

"Did Piyush ever mention his sister Latika?"

"Yes."

"She is not here today but you should meet her. I think you both would look great together."

"Oh, thank you but-" I was interrupted by Piyush's father before I could respond.

"Let's take a breather here. Kaveri, maybe we can get into it over dinner when Piyush is here."

"OK. OK. I'm not imposing anything on poor KK here. A mother can worry about her daughter, can't she? We don't need to involve Piyush in this discussion yet," Kaveri said, as dinner was getting served. We all sat on the floor with our legs crossed to eat daal roti out of stainless-steel plates. After dinner Piyush's parents left for their hotel. Piyush and I went out for a stroll in the now closed market.

"Piyush, my mind has been all over the place and with you being so well-read and wise, I need your honest opinion about something."

"Only honest feedback is available, KK."

"Do you think Mira and I stand a fighting chance? I wonder if what we have is realistic. Her sister doesn't fully approve of us; her parents don't even know about us yet. And now, I am running thousands of miles away for school so I can win the approval of Bina and their parents."

"I haven't exactly cracked that code for myself yet, but I do have a question for you. How much to do you love Mira?"

"She means more to me than words can express."

"Then take it one day at a time, assuming each day with her in your life is better than a day without her. Do your best with what you can control."

"What if I bypassed Bina and went straight to Mira's parents?"

"Well, you can imagine all the questions that would come up. How accomplished are your parents? How educated are you? How will you provide for a family with Mira? An American degree can help sidestep all those concerns."

"How will I pay for that degree?"

"Beg. Borrow. Steal. And then, let the visa gods work their magic."

"Say all that works out, how will I stay away from Mira for two years?"

"There are people who go to war or prison and stay away from family longer than that. And graduate school goes faster than you think."

"I don't know if I have it in me."

***

As I veered away from the main road on to a smaller street, the moped's brake handle flew off. I saw that the fork ahead of me contained three branches. I quickly glanced at the map mounted on the handle and none of the routes were highlighted. I looked back and the broken brake handle was lying in the middle of the street, and it was quickly receding. Stop? Turn back? Keep going?

I woke up in panic on a train ride that seemed never-ending. I was back in Star City. I couldn't imagine facing a visa officer without proof of funds. Piyush's advice to beg, borrow, or steal to pay for graduate school was still fresh in my mind.

I stepped down from the autorickshaw and was paying the driver, when mom stepped out to help with my bags. She muttered, "Aunt Lakshmi and Uncle Mohan are here to meet you."

"Why? How did they know when I was getting home?" I fumed. The first thing I needed was a long shower. Oh, and did I mention the bags of money needed right after?

"Go shower. We can talk over lunch. We will wait," Aunt Lakshmi said when I walked in.

"Where is dad?"

"He stepped out as soon as we walked in," Uncle Mohan noted.

CHAPTER 4: BORROWED STRENGTH

I didn't want the shower to end. But I knew the hot water wouldn't last forever. I wished Piyush was here, helping me respond to whatever Aunt Lakshmi was here to confront me with. Or this could be an interesting test for how much of his wisdom had truly rubbed off on me.

Over rice and lentils, the small talk about differences between Delhi and Star City never seemed to end.

"Is that a deodorant you bought in Delhi? Is it imported? Smells good," Aunt Lakshmi remarked.

"We will get some mango pickle for you when it's time to leave for America. It will be packaged well for international travel and should last you for months."

I couldn't help but wonder where this was going.

"Aunt Lakshmi, I only have an admission notification for now, there is a lot more-" I was finishing my thought before I was cut off mid-sentence.

"Oh, I'm sure the visa will not be a problem, and you will be first from our family to set foot on US soil," beamed Aunt Lakshmi, "and we can help finance your studies."

I gasped. And in the process swallowed the half-chewed food. I reached for a glass of water.

"We want to see you succeed. This home is still in my mother's name and I'm sure it is enough for collateral. Uncle Mohan's brother works at

The Union Bank, and he will act as a guarantor. Banks are eager to lend in these situations; it is good business for them. But we have a small request," Aunt Lakshmi continued.

The next bite paused before it hit my mouth. Truly, where could this conversation be going?

"You know how your cousin Venkat looks up to you and has always wanted to go to America. We want you to mentor him once you get to the States, but there is something else you could help resolve while you're here."

"How can I help?"

"Venkat liked a girl in college from a different caste. They got along well for a while, but she abruptly cut off all communication. He has been a wreck for a few months. We want you to put some sense into his head."

"Why can't we wait to see if the situation resolves by itself? My intervention could make things worse."

"If anything, things have been getting worse. He is locked in his room all the time. His grades have hit rock bottom, and we're worried he may not graduate on time," Uncle Mohan chimed in. "You know how stubborn he is, we are hoping he will listen to you. Dangle the carrot of a future in America as much as possible."

My immediate thought was to ask if they had considered professional help. But I held back. If they considered the idea a taboo, I didn't want to risk upsetting them.

"Sure, I will do what I can," I said, withholding cough. I felt queasy.

I called Mira from a nearby phone booth the same evening.

"How was day 1?" she inquired.

"I'm feeling funny, maybe it's something I ate on the train. Other than that, full of surprises. The money part might work out after all!"

"Slow down, meanie! Are you in a rush to get away from me?"

"Come away with me! We can build a cottage in the middle of nowhere and live happily ever after," I proposed.

"America is just a layover. I'm your destination. You are fully committed now."

"That will work too. Pray to the visa gods for me. Now tell me something about you."

"Mom and dad think they should move to Delhi to be closer to Bina and me beginning next year."

"No more back and forth between Lucknow and Delhi for you then!"

"It's all plans right now, let's see what time has in store for us. When you get back to India, you're moving to where I am too, no excuses."

"That goes without saying, architects are needed everywhere."

"Come join us for dinner, KK. Mom made your favorite tamarind rice and fried potatoes," dad said, as he let me in.

I saw him after months. His forehead showed a few more wrinkles. The dark circles under his eyes were much more prominent now. His shoulders seemed burdened by his thin frame. I touched his feet and hugged him tight.

"Dad, are you taking care of yourself?"

"Sure, why? You know I'm as tough as they come," he assured. "How has Delhi treated you? I see you've become much leaner."

"I missed you guys. It's a tough world when you must fend for yourself," I responded.

"Let's have dinner together, I want to make the most of it while you're in Star City."

"I'm don't have much of an appetite dad, why don't you leave the food on the table and I will eat later?" I said, not mentioning how even a five-course gourmet meal felt like too much of an effort.

I got up in the middle of the night and felt the world spin around me.

I dreamed about sharing some laughs with Mira, mom, and dad. Not sure what the joke was or what was so funny about it. But the sight of Mira laughing was so easy on the eyes. I could go to the end of the world and come back for that laughter. And was that a crimson bindi between her eyebrows? Why was she wearing it now when she didn't do it in the past despite my begging for it literally? Were we married in this dream? The human mind sure has a way of making up things it desires. Or so I thought.

"Can you hear me love? When are you going to wake up? Maybe he is not ready yet."

"How much longer are you going to keep us waiting?"

"Just tell me once you're doing all right!"

I opened my eyes slowly, squinting to avoid the piercing daylight. After the full view of a revolving ceiling fan I had never seen before, the first thing I felt was a warm hand on mine and the reassuring smile of Mira. She was wearing a bindi, so I must have still been dreaming. With her eyes fixed on mine, her lips figuring out the right words to say, and her warm palm cupping my knuckles, I wished the dream never ended.

"Welcome back, sweetheart! It's just you and me here!" Mira said with her smile intact.

"I feel like a feather floating in space. Maybe it's your presence?"

"The fever and other symptoms have subsided but you're still weak. Don't move your left arm too much, you're still on the IV drip."

"What happened? How long was I out? Where are mom and dad?"

"Mom and dad were here all night. They went home to shower and get a few things for you. I arrived yesterday but I believe today is your sixth day in the hospital. The doctors suspect it started as food poisoning but given your respiratory symptoms, they also suspect pneumonia. You're too fragile for 36-hour train journeys."

"Oh wow! And I managed to drag you into this mess?"

"Well, you didn't call for three days in a row and I got worried!"

"How did you track me down?"

"That is a long story for another time. You seem to be on the mend and that's what matters."

"Now that you're here, let's make some plans!"

"I will have to cancel the dinner reservation because the doctors say it might be a two more days before you're back on home cooked food," Mira chuckled softly.

"Did you know you were smiling a lot in your sleep?"

"I was dreaming of America."

"I won't give you a tough time about that, but I will be leaving for my flight shortly. I need to get home before nightfall."

"Please stay longer."

"I wish I could. Even this overnight trip wasn't easy to pull off. Get some rest and recover fully for our next meeting."

"When will that be?"

"Why don't you fly out of Delhi, and we can spend some time together before you leave for America?"

"That's a good idea."

"I have to go but mom and dad should be back soon," Mira said while closing my eyes with her palm.

***

I lost two precious weeks in recovery. Time, tide, and visa gods wait for none. But there were two profound revelations for me in these few weeks. My waking up after being so severely ill felt miraculous. I had checked out of this world for almost a week with nothing to show but a few lucid dreams. I could have easily kept going and never returned. Is this calm before a bigger storm or have I been set free? The cherry on top was Mira's visit demonstrating her commitment to me.

First thing to check off the to-do list was dealing with Venkat's obsession.

"You're so lucky to have someone like Mira. Don't I deserve my own Mira?" he argued.

"When you find her, she will run in your direction, not away from you," I countered.

"If I get one conversation with Shanti, I can put some sense into her head. But I'm sure her brother won't let that happen! Our principal is not helping either. He tells me I can't write to her, call her, or get within twenty feet of her."

"What if Shanti herself said she wouldn't want to hear from you again?”

“That’s impossible! As earth shattering as that may be, I would want to hear her say it! I would also want to know why!”

“I can call her brother for one supervised meeting if you agree with two things. She does not owe you an explanation, or her viewpoint may not match yours. Either way you will take a no gracefully.”

Next day at the same time, we were sitting inside a beachfront coffee shop and waiting for Shanti to arrive with her brother.

“They’re late. I’ll give it another five minutes,” I observed.

“I see they’re parking their motorcycle,” Venkat said, trying to conceal a smile.

I walked up to the brother, introduced myself and asked if we could hang out at a distance while Venkat and Shanti spoke. He nodded and Shanti walked away from us.

“It’s highly unlikely we will see each other again. Is there anything you want to get off your chest?” he muttered.

“What is the hold up? Aren’t they both adults who can think for themselves?” I inquired.

“We’re from a conservative community. We don’t let our girls wander. Maybe you should take Venkat to Delhi with you so he can find someone there.”

“I wish it were that simple. The heart wants what it wants, don’t you think?”

“I’m confident Shanti will side with us. We’re not averse to physically ripping hearts out of chests, if that is what it takes. You will be lucky to find Venkat’s body if he persists.”

Before I knew it, I was holding the guy’s wrist, softly at first as if to beg for mercy but the grip quickly tightened.

He wiggled.

He tried to pull away.

He tried to undo my grip with his left hand.

I did not lower my gaze; I did not let go. “Take back what you said and apologize.”

“What? Let go, you crazy idiot!”

"You heard me. We can be here all day!" I yelled.

I felt a tap on my shoulder. "We're done here," Venkat whispered.

"I hope we don't see each other again because Venkat is hurt," I muttered as I let go.

"You're going to pay for this!" Shanti's brother muttered back as he walked out rubbing his wrist. Shanti followed him closely.

"Thanks for being there," said Venkat as he shook my right hand and wiped his tears with his left.

"Of course."

***

Uncle Mohan and I were sitting across from the bank manager in his office at The Union Bank of Star City.

"Everything checks out. We will release 25% of the loan each semester. This is an easy loan because I'm guessing you're not coming back for the second installment."

"Why do you say that?" I asked.

"Who knows? It has happened before. One last formality though. You will have to get your property appraised. Here's the business card of the appraiser. He will be visiting you at home this afternoon for a walk-through. And you can collect your check soon after we receive the appraisal."

The appraiser first walked around the outside of the building and then checked the interiors.

He took a sip from his cup of tea that mom placed in front of him and said, "Real estate has been on the up and up in the city generally, but this neighborhood hasn't kept up. I can work backwards from your loan amount and let you fill in an amount of your choice for a small off-the-books price. I will be going out on a limb here, so I hope you understand."

Mom teared up. Dad got up and paced back and forth. Was there no good deed that went unpunished? There was not much valuable left in the house to pawn. I could imagine a life without America. If I didn't have Mira, there wouldn't be much else to lose.

"Have you heard of Taekwondo, sir?" I inquired.

"Is that martial arts? Why, are you an expert?"

"I'm just a student but there are five tenets. Courtesy, Integrity, Perseverance, Self-control, and Indomitable Spirit, sir. I think I will be OK with four of them, but I don't know if I will ever be able to master self-control."

"What does that have to do with anything?"

"Two weeks ago, I almost died. The other day, I almost broke someone's arm because they threatened my cousin's life. So, whatever self-control I had in me seems to be slowly slipping away. I know the house has some deferred maintenance issues, but between the value of the land and the house, I'm hoping we're covered. You can turn in the appraisal as you see fit. If there is nothing else to discuss, I hope you enjoyed the tea."

The appraiser seemed disoriented for a minute. Then he scribbled something on his notepad and left. We received a call the next morning that the loan was approved.

***

As the train slowed down in the Delhi station, I saw Piyush through the window and waved as he walked along.

He hugged me tightly and whispered, "Welcome back, I missed you!"

"I missed you too. I feel like I have aged years in the past few weeks. I could have used your wisdom during several situations back home."

"Oh, you're being too generous!"

In no time we were in an autorickshaw.

"You've lost weight, how are you feeling now?"

"Getting back to full strength. How have you been? What did I miss?"

"Only some rain and a few power outages. Did you manage to get a visa interview appointment?"

"Yes, the appointment is in a week. I have no idea what to expect."

"Imagine the visa has already been approved and you're just going there to collect paperwork. I'm sure you will do fine."

"I'll be waiting for you right here in this cafe, you go get'em," Piyush said, as I got off the Vespa and handed the helmet to him.

"Wish me luck."

"You don't need it! Remember, you're only going to collect the papers, the decision has already been made. Don't do anything I wouldn't!"

In Delhi, tall compound walls with fortified gates were not an uncommon sight. Because the actual building was not often visible from the outside, the design of the wall and the gate tend to become fashion statements in themselves. Some even had planter beds on the outside to help humanize the scale. But this one was a bland beige wall with barbed wire fencing atop. Two guards in uniforms outside the black gate cracked it open to let people in, one at a time. The gold-plated lettering on the wall read "Embassy of The United States of America." The line meandered across the street and into an adjoining tree-lined street, a good two hundred feet maybe. Some stood anxiously while others perched on the sidewalk and curbs with family members. The roads in all directions were barricaded to block any through traffic. It was overcast at 7 a.m. with a slight nip in the air. I joined at the end of the line.

"The embassy doesn't open until 8 a.m. Half these people will be turned away because they are too early for their appointment. When is yours?" said the guy ahead of me in the line, shaking his head.

"9:15, yours?" I engaged hesitantly.

"10 o'clock. It's tough out there, too many visa applications getting rejected. Is that what you're hearing too?"

"I don't know man. My friends who went to study all left last year."

"This is my second attempt. I'm hoping it works this time."

"Good luck, to you and to me," I replied.

"What is your plan B?"

I tried to speak but my voice gave out. "Listen man, I feel for you, but can we talk about something else?" I blurted. My heart was beating like a drum, and it felt like my body parts could collapse into a heap. I closed my eyes. I inhaled slowly through my nose, filled up my abdomen, and exhaled through my mouth. Just as they taught us in our Taekwondo classes. And I kept repeating it.

As the entrance gate neared, we could see people exiting through an adjacent gate. Only blank faces and shaking heads so far. No pumping fists or ear-to-ear smiles.

"Appointment confirmation, please?" said the guard as he ushered the guy in front of me through the door.

"Walk toward that door and you can keep your shoes on when going through the metal detector," the guard pointed.

After a slight walk on a paved pathway surrounded by grass and vegetation, and passing through the antechamber, we were in a lobby where front desk personnel checked everyone's paperwork and put them in the right order. Through a glass door, I could see folks standing in lines parallel to each other, facing their respective counters.

"Here's your stuff, you can go join the line for counter 6."

The orderliness and efficiency were a sight to behold. If this set up was a microcosm of America, travelers will need a lifestyle change to get used to it.

There were about a dozen people ahead of me at counter 6. Some lines were moving faster than the others.

At counter number 5, there was a couple in traditional south Indian attire who seemed to be having trouble with their interview. I could only hear things faintly as all the conversations were a big jumble.

"Sir, we are only going there to visit our son for a month, why can't you-"

And then came a booming voice from across the counter that you couldn't miss if you tried. "You do your job and let me do mine! Do not tell me how to do my job!" Everyone watched with their mouths wide open as the dispirited couple walked toward the exit.

Eventually it was my turn at the counter.

"Hey, I'm Jeff. Can you say your name for me, please?"

"Hello, Jeff. My name is Krishna Kant Sharma. You can call me KK."

"I see that you are intending to pursue graduate studies. Why Scottsdale Institute of Technology?"

"The program there comes highly recommended from friends."

"Why is higher education important to you?"

"Architects like me are dime a dozen here. I need specialization to stand out and build a good career."

"Let me see your passport and I-20."

"Here it is," I said passing the documents through the depression in the counter.

Jeff started at the documents intently, followed by some intense keyboard typing.

"Who will be paying for your education?"

"My parents and my grandmother."

There were more sounds of keyboard clicks.

"Are you a Muslim?"

I froze. Nobody warned me about this. Was this relevant? Should I be bothered about where this was going?

"Focus on collecting the documents, no distractions!" I could hear Piyush whispering in my ear. I collected myself quickly.

"I'm not, Jeff."

"Do you practice Islam?"

"Laser focus!" I could hear Piyush repeating.

"I don't, Jeff."

"Pardon my ignorance," Jeff said, glancing to the right at his monitor.

Jeff flipped through all the pages of the passport and set it aside before returning my I-20. "See those guys at the front desk? They will send your passport back to you."

"Sorry, what does that mean? Is my visa approved?"

"You're all set!"

For a moment, the cosmos felt like a just place. "Cheer up, you deserve this," I told myself. As I stepped out, it felt like I was walking on foam.

Piyush was waiting right outside the exit gate. He started beaming as I walked out half unconscious. He started jumping up and down.

"The son of a gun did it!" Piyush blurted.

"I feel like the dog that caught the car!"

"Stop with that modesty. It's time to celebrate!"

"It wouldn't have been possible without you!"

"Oh, stop it!"

Little did Piyush realize that I meant that literally. His advice to walk in for collecting already approved papers served its purpose.

On the way home, we stopped at a phone booth to call Mira. I decided to have some fun with the process.

"Hey love, I've been by the phone all this time, I can't wait to hear how it went."

I paused intentionally. "I have some good news and bad news. Which one do you want first?" I said with a somber tone.

Again, things went quiet for a few seconds.

"Are you being serious? Just lay it on me." I could hear Mira's voice breaking.

"I see what happened as a sign that I wasn't meant to be away from you for two full years," I continued, with the same somber tone.

"You're on speaker. Bina wants to say something."

"Hey Bina, sorry you're having to hear this."

"We thought you were well prepared. What happened?"

"I think they are on edge in the aftermath of 9/11. I was not alone. I noticed too many denials."

"What are you going to do now?"

"I'm still processing it. Maybe we just tell your parents that I tried but it didn't work."

"Oh, that's not going to fly. And my sister must still finish her master's program."

"What if we just eloped?"

"That would decimate our family. And I want nothing but the grandest wedding for Mira. No shortcuts, no workarounds."

I could hear Mira asking for the phone back in the background, but Bina persisted.

"I think we should all take a break and figure out the best course forward."

"How long of a break do you think?"

"As long as it takes."

"We have a problem then," I countered.

"He is just messing with you guys!" Piyush blurted from behind with a chuckle.

"You troublemaker! You just gave me the scare of my life, KK!" Mira erupted.

"Sorry about that. When will I see you?"

"I'm coming over! Don't make any plans! We must make the most of your remaining time in India."

"I needed to hear that."

***

"I'm happy for you but in the remaining four months, I need you to finish detailing the Garden Terraces project. It's a challenge to get people to stick around these days. Spread the word and help us find your replacement," Nishkam instructed.

Garden Terraces was a luxury apartment project where each apartment had its own shaded terrace to walk out into. The street facing elevation of the project looked like a checkerboard with alternating residential units and terraces. Circular staircases connected by floating walkways leading to main entries abutted the courtyard facing elevation. Landscape design was central to visually tying all the open spaces together. Oriented to utilize cool breezes for passive ventilation, the high-rise project was the first of its kind in the Delhi metro area. Ashish and I burned the midnight oil with the help of countless cups of chai so he could take the finished drawings on his next site visit. I was sure going to miss seeing the project come to fruition in construction.

"You're one lucky dude to get the visa, did you know that? Denials are not uncommon but lately that is all you hear about," Ashish remarked while hunched over his drawing board one evening.

"I think so too. It feels unreal. It's almost unfair to the other qualified people facing denials."

"Agreed. I have several friends who got admissions but were denied visas. After a denial, it gets harder. In my wife's case, the officer accused her of being desperate to immigrate to the USA and asked her to not bother trying again. I didn't mention it before because I didn't want to discourage you."

"That's preposterous. I wonder how they arrive at that conclusion."

"Explaining their decision is not their strong suit. I think the onus to demonstrate strong ties to India is on the applicant. No customer service, no refunds."

"What about the paper they hand you at the end of the visa interview? It must have had some useful feedback?"

"That's just a boiler plate checklist. Not useful at all."

"How did your wife take it?"

"It was a long time ago. She is over it now but the damage from your intentions getting questioned never fully goes away."

"Well, I'm coming back no matter what. I don't have a choice."

"We will leave a spot open for you here, assuming we can afford you that is," Ashish chuckled.

"That is kind of you."

"How is Mira taking all this?"

"Very well, I think."

"They say distance makes the heart grow fonder, but distance also makes things challenging, you know?"

"Our bond is strong. We will wait it out."

"I like your confidence. Keep the faith. When are you seeing her next?"

"We're in touch over the phone. She is working on dates to visit. And it's not like I have spare time. I'm asking her to visit in early August. That way, we can spend two full weeks together before I fly out."

"Tell her I expect her to keep her end of the bargain."

"I will. Thank you."

***

The expression 'time flies' no longer felt abstract when end of July arrived. Nishkam and Ashish took a few of us out to lunch to bid me farewell. I felt like the last twelve months had given me the life experience and courage needed to stare into the abyss that lay ahead. After all the hugs and teary goodbyes, I headed straight to the train station to receive Mira.

As I entered the station, it started raining lightly. I could hear the announcer on the loudspeaker, "Travelers, please pay attention. Paschim Express arriving from Lucknow will be arriving an hour late, on platform number five instead of platform number one." The announcement kept repeating every few minutes. To kill time, I started browsing at the store on the platform. There were rows of books and discs. I had started packing my bags and they were already getting full. So, I didn't need more weight. It occurred to me that I should buy something for Mira. In Piyush's absence, I turned to the vendor for recommendations.

"I can only tell you what we sell a lot of," he remarked as he slid a few things toward me. Based on the descriptions on the back, I chose a book titled The World According to Garp and discs of movies titled Jerry Maguire and Point Break.

"Are these legitimate, will they work like they should?" I inquired about the discs.

"Don't waste my time, take it or leave it," the vendor snapped.

"I'll take them."

As the train's arrival time neared, I took the stairs to the pedestrian bridge to get to platform five.

When Paschim Express initially approached the platform, it felt like it was never going to stop. As it slowed down, I eagerly looked at the windows and doors for a glimpse of Mira. I thought I caught a glimpse, but the compartment sped away so I followed along on the platform until the train came to a full stop. It was Mira but she looked very different. As she got down the steps and we walked toward each other, she might as well have been a model from one of the magazine covers. The embrace was warm but short-lived to avoid attracting attention.

"You smell good," Mira observed.

"Thanks. You look stunning," I countered.

"How are you doing?"

"The last hour was harder to kill than the last few weeks. You?"

"I could say the same about the last ten hours. Sorry the train was behind schedule."

Then Mira said something that startled me.

"I think you didn't spot me on the train because you were looking at other women."

"Of all the women on that train, you're the most beautiful one."

"You're lying."

"It's the truth. Your hair and eyebrows are so different, it wasn't easy to spot you."

"I wanted to look my best for you, so I tried a different beauty parlor."

"It worked."

"Oh, thanks. What's that in the bag?" Mira inquired, swiftly changing gears.

"A little something to remind you of me, while I'm away. When we meet after the next break, you must tell me how you like them," I replied, handing her the plastic bag with the book and the discs.

"Sure. Are you hungry?" Mira asked, as she browsed through the contents.

"Famished!"

"Let's head to that Italian place in Vasant Vihar!"

"Tuscan Delight? In the PVR Complex?"

"Yes, that one."

By now, rain had picked up.

"Do you want to get there by a cab? I don't want you to get wet."

"I'd rather be with you on the Vespa," Mira said with a big grin.

I went back to the store to get a couple of ponchos.

"These are legitimate," the vendor quipped, with a sarcastic smile.

With the poncho, I handed Mira the spare helmet. We were on our way. Traffic was light. The Vespa held up like a champ despite the weather. The rain had let up by the time we got to the restaurant.

"You and me in the rain, the best scooter ride of my life," Mira observed as we pulled up.

"Mine too," I said with an ear-to-ear smile.

"Get used to it, this is a glimpse of your future."

As we waited for the food to arrive, Mira's right hand was in my left hand. Soon, we were exchanging bites of spaghetti and lasagna.

"How was the train journey?"

"It felt too long but no other hitches. When do you fly out?"

"In two weeks. I have a question for you."

"Tell me."

"Are you really worried that I'm looking at other women?"

"Oh, that. Don't worry about it."

"I'd rather know now if it is bothering you."

"I thought our eyes had met briefly but you didn't recognize me. And we're going to be apart for so long, how do I know you will not meet someone in America?"

"If you met someone here while I'm gone, will you leave me?"

"You're making this about me instead of answering my question," Mira shot back.

"I'm just trying to tell you that your fear is irrational."

"You don't understand what I'm trying to say," Mira said, holding back tears. She got up and walked.

"Where are you going?"

She walked straight into the women's washroom. I wanted to but couldn't follow her in there. I waited outside the door, a few feet away.

My heart was racing. So was my mind. The food suddenly lost all its flavor. The restaurant lighting that I hadn't even noticed until then started hurting my eyes. How could I have hurt the person I loved? Did I even deserve Mira's love?

Mira walked out, held my hand and led us back to our table.

"I'm so sorry! I didn't realize I was being hurtful!" I offered, trying to lock eyes with her.

"It's OK. Maybe I'm losing my mind at the prospect of not being able to see you whenever I want to. And to be honest, I am worried about you finding someone else. What if you never returned to India again? Did I mention that I was cheated on before?"

"I'm so sorry you had to go through that; I had no idea. Obviously, I'm a fool for not being empathetic and patient with you, for not trusting your intuition and asking you to explain further. But, what kind of a fool would lose someone like you?"

"Someone I cared about deeply."

"You know where I'm going to study, right? For the next two years, you know where to find me. You can corner me anytime about anything. Just like you're doing right now. I will call you regularly. When calls get too expensive, my emails will be so long that they will put you to sleep. And I promise, I will always be loyal to you, until my last breath. Can I ask you for the same in return?"

"I promise. That is all I wanted to hear. Thank you," Mira relented.

"Sorry to interrupt sir but the kitchen is closing. Any last-minute orders you want to put in?" the waiter asked.

I looked around and we were the only patrons left. The crew had already begun to stack the chairs upside down on the tables.

"That will be all. Check please!"

CHAPTER 5: FOLLOW HEART OR MIND?

Two weeks. That's how long I had left with Mira. Before getting on an airplane for the first time and crossing oceans and continents. Before leaving the love of my life behind. And if the evening I received Mira from the train station taught me anything, love can be long lasting and fragile at the same time.

The next day we met in Alaknanda Market, near the same medical store that introduced us to each other.

"How is Piyush doing now?" Mira asked.

"He is all right. I don't know what kind of roommates I will get in the US but I'm going to miss him."

"What's better than one long distance relationship? Two long distance relationships," Mira chuckled.

"When do you think we will meet again?"

"Unlike here, I hear America has breaks for every season. We should print your school's calendar and mark your future visits up."

"Do you think you will be able to visit me sometime?"

"That's ambitious. I'm yet to apply for a passport."

"What?"

"Little did I suspect I will fall in love with such a globetrotter!"

"That should be first thing on your to do list then. Maybe I can save enough to buy you a ticket for winter break."

"Speaking of travel, I have a surprise for you."

"Bring it on."

"You and I are going to Vaishno Devi day after tomorrow."

"Are you talking about the shrine near Jammu?"

"Yes."

"Are you asking me or telling me?" I couldn't hide feeling blindsided.

"Both."

"And why are we doing that?"

"To get Mata's blessings for your trip and our future together."

I was at a loss for words. I was not averse to religious rituals and gestures, but I never had the patience to sit through even an hour-long ceremony. The upside was Mira and I would get to spend quality uninterrupted time together for almost a week.

"Can we not go to a local shrine here and get the blessings?"

"Yes, we can, but it's not the same thing. We need the next level blessing for our situation."

"Is Bina going along?"

"No."

"How did you convince her to stay out of it?"

"She is not that bad, she can be understanding. She only wants what is best for me."

"What about travel and hotel reservations?"

"It's all taken care of. You will be back well in time for your flight. And I know how you fell sick during your travel home recently, so we will only eat at the best places and drink bottled water throughout the trip."

"It sounds like you have thought this through, and you make a compelling case."

"Pack your bags then, we have less than 48 hours."

We left early for the bus depot, and we were well on our way to Jammu by the time sun rose and made it out of the clouds. The first half of the ride was relatively smooth. We stopped for lunch. The second half was hilly terrain with torrential downpour. What would have been scenic views were completely obscured by windows draped by rain. We could feel the twists and turns as the bus navigated what felt like treacherous ghat roads. There was no doubt that all speed limits were ignored. I woke up to an intense thump and clutched Mira's hand.

"What a cliffhanger of a ride. I hope we make it there alive," I whispered in Mira's ear.

"We're almost there. They say nobody gets to visit without Mata's invitation. This is our test."

"Do you really believe all that?"

"Absolutely. Trips planned for months get canceled at the last minute. And last-minute plans go smoothly. It's all up to Mata's divine blessings."

"Wow, I didn't realize you were such a believer."

"Let's make the most of this."

The bus ride came to a final halt at Jammu. As we lined up to get down, we could hear commotion and saw a crowd gathered around a small group of people. As we walked toward the exit, it became clear that a big gnarly looking guy was kicking a woman who was initially standing but fell to the ground under the blows. There was a guy next to the fallen woman on his knees begging the big guy to spare them. But the big guy continued to kick the woman in her stomach.

"I think I need to go help them, the poor lady is getting battered," I said as we stepped down from the bus.

"We need to catch the next bus to Katra. Don't get distracted."

"What if the woman dies? She is already bleeding at the mouth."

"Did you see how strong that guy is? What do you hope to accomplish?"

"Everyone is watching a show, and nobody is intervening. Even if the lady is at fault, do you think she deserves that treatment?"

"I don't want you to get hurt. And if you get involved with a police matter, your international travel could get jeopardized."

"What is the issue?" I asked a bystander.

"The guy is selling bus seats on the black market and the couple refused to move from the seats he had blocked out. The lady wouldn't stop arguing with him."

"If you love me, you will not do anything," I could hear Mira yelling as I walked into the crowd.

I made my way through to the front and got in between the big guy and the lady.

"What are you doing?"

"Unless you're paying for their seats, get out of the way," he muttered as he held me by my shirt and pushed me so hard that I landed on my butt with my back against the legs of the crowd. Distracted, he spat out whatever he was chewing and turned toward the lady on the ground.

I got up with my fist clenched, paced toward him, sprung up in the air and landed a firm elbow blow on his cheek. The guy slumped to the ground like a pile of boneless flesh, hunched over and disoriented.

"I think he broke his jaw," someone yelled.

I looked for Mira. There she was, standing at a distance, expressionless, and her shoulders stiff like I had never seen before. Then she turned around, crossed the lane, and sat down on a bench under a canopy.

The crowd began dispersing. Someone said the police were coming. Someone else laughed. The couple in distress picked up their scattered belongings on their way out. I clutched my elbow and walked to Mira. I sat next to her, my palms on my knees, and my feet drawn under the seat of the bench.

The silence was punctuated by buses passing by, idling engines, and the crunching of plastic water bottles in people's hands. Mira removed a hand kerchief from her purse and wiped her palms and face, as if she was brushing off the air around her.

"I told you," she whispered under her breath.

I know. I tried. You were right. Several thoughts crossed my mind, but I did not say anything.

"It's hard to be in love with someone who's hospitalized or jailed, you know?"

"I wasn't thinking," I muttered.

"You don't get to make these decisions by yourself, especially when I'm with you."

"I'm sorry," I said, hating how half-hearted it sounded.

The cop who was at the scene made his way to us.

"Are you the guy who was in the skirmish?"

"Yes, sir."

"Do you have a penchant for violence?"

"No, sir."

"Do you need medical assistance?"

"I'm OK. Thank you."

"The guy is a known miscreant, and he is not pressing charges. You guys look like tourists. You should get going and stay out of trouble."

We hailed a cab and set out to Katra.

When we got to the hotel, we walked in as if we were there separately. We sat down on a couch in the lobby.

"Listen," I tried. My elbow was still throbbing.

"Not right now. Not today. I need time to understand what this costs me," Mira responded, staring at the drapes on the windows.

"Shall we check in?"

"I had reserved one room for us. We need to add a second."

The next morning, we were at the entry point bright and early. The view of the Trikuta Mountains was breathtaking. Thus began the 14-mile trek for a glimpse of Mata Rani, with utter silence between us. I knew I hadn't lost Mira, not yet, but there was an unknown price to be paid for normalcy that may never be the same again.

We stopped at the holy river Banganga for a dip.

Then we stopped at Charan Paduka to touch the imprints of what were believed to be the goddess' feet.

We took breaks at Adhkuwari and Sanjichhat.

The final viewing location for Mata Rani was a walk through a cave-like structure. The line moved quickly. There were no elaborate idols or frames. There were three natural rock formations decorated with jewelry and clothing. We bowed to offer our prayers.

"Give me the wisdom to never take Mira for granted again," I prayed on the inside, with my hands folded.

We were asked to move along by the usher to make space for folks next in the line.

As we stepped out, I made eye contact with Mira after what felt like a long while.

"I think that went well, how do you feel?"

"At peace."

"Did you forget to offer those garlands at the sanctum?"

"I need them for something else."

"If that was the last stop, shall we begin the descent?"

"We're not done yet. There is a Shiva Temple a couple of kilometers further up. But I need to talk to you about something before we head up."

This must be a good sign, right? She is feeling at peace and wants to complete the full pilgrimage. I could sense she was going through an inner dialog though. And what better place than this to resolve everything?

"I'm tired. Can't we talk on our way down?"

"The trip is considered complete only after the visit to the Shiva Temple."

"OK, then. What's going on in that head of yours?"

"How much do you love me?"

"Excuse me?" I uttered, caught off guard.

"I need to know how much you love me."

I hugged her tightly and whispered in her ear, "words can never fully express how much I love you."

"Thank you. I feel the same way about you. Will you marry me?"

I was physically already on top of the world but now I felt giddy. The throbbing in the elbow suddenly disappeared. Gods granted wishes but I didn't know miracles happened while temple visits were still in progress.

"Of course, I would. And here I was thinking you would never talk to me again after last evening. We have two years to plan a wedding, let us plan a good one."

"Let me rephrase, will you marry me at the Shiva Temple in 30 minutes?"

I felt the ground slipping from under my feet. The heights that felt exhilarating until then now felt dizzying.

"I don't understand. Do you not want me to go to America?"

"You should still go."

"Why the rush? What about our families and doing things right by them?" I wondered aloud.

"They can wait. This is just for you and me, our little secret. This way, I know you're always mine, even when you are at a distance. No matter how long it takes for us to reunite. Everything you do from here on is for both of us. I know I'm asking for a lot, but I hope you'll understand."

"When did you realize you wanted this?"

"That does not matter. All that matters now is if you want this too or not."

"What if I ran away and never came back?"

"I will come find you, wherever you are hiding."

I sat down on the stairs right there. She was my person but was the timing right? If this was the right thing to do, why the short notice? Why hide it from the world? How long would we have to stay apart after getting married? What if I said no? Seconds turned into minutes.

"So, will you marry me?"

My innards were twisting like a coil, both with excitement and anxiety. It is what I wanted anyway, just a little sooner than I thought, I told myself.

"My heart says yes," I said, leaving out the part that my mind was undecided.

Accompanied by a chanting priest, we exchanged garlands, I applied vermilion in her hair parting above her forehead and tied the sacred thread around her neck.

After the ceremony, we were a married couple.

Back in Katra, we went straight to a photo studio for pictures. We paid extra to put a rush on the prints. "One copy for you and one copy for me," Mira said with a gleeful smile.

***

It was finally the day before taking off for America. Mom and dad visited Delhi to see me off. Mom somehow found a way to stuff my luggage with a brand-new pressure cooker filled with uncooked rice, just in case food was hard to find the first few days.

"Mom, America is anything but an impoverished nation. There will be plenty of food there," I protested.

"You can never be too careful. I also want you to wear this gold ring of dad that you can sell in case of an emergency."

I tried it and it was too small on the ring finger and too big for the little finger.

"It's not the right fit mom; I don't want to lose it."

"Have you tried both hands? I will ask dad to go to the jewelry store to get it resized."

"I don't want dad wandering the streets of Delhi looking for a goldsmith. It's too late for that."

"Just put it in your wallet then. You can get it resized in America," mom concluded.

"I know you know this but don't forget to send monthly interest payments on time," dad reminded.

"Eat on time and write or call regularly," were mom's last words before I walked past security into the airport gates.

"Apply for passports as soon as you get back to Star City," were my last words as I waved back.

One of my favorite architects, I. M. Pei, observed that when you traveled the world, you owned the world.

The unknown always excited me but this felt very different. As the flight took off, dad's alcoholism, mom's holding the dam from breaking, and the desperation from witnessing Piyush under attack were all in the background now. The armpit wound from the knife attack had healed. The elbow pain from the bus station was almost gone. But I was carrying something far heavier with me. Even if it was the best kept secret, I was married now, and in Mira, I was leaving a part of me behind.

When the flight started descending into Dubai airport, my ears hurt as if someone was hammering nails into them simultaneously from both sides. I was too disabled and too embarrassed to turn to fellow passengers and ask for help. As painful as it was, the physical pain momentarily masked the emotional burden from pretending everything was fine.

During the layover, I used the internet at the airport to look for a remedy for ear pain. Chewing gum, swallowing or popping your ears with your nose closed were the suggested remedies.

CHAPTER 6: ARRIVAL WITHOUT ANCHORS

The second take off from Dubai to Phoenix was full of comforts. Good food, coffee, blankets, and entertainment on the consoles. But that photograph, the only evidence of our wedding, in my bag in the overhead bin with my passport and other documents, weighed on me heavily.

I got my first lesson in airplane etiquette when a fellow passenger tapped on the arm of an attendant to get his attention and was swiftly admonished with a "please don't touch me sir, how can I help you?"

At Phoenix airport, there were two different lines to the immigration check in. One for visitors. The other for permanent residents and citizens.

"Hello, sir," I greeted the officer across the counter with a glass wall handing my passport and other forms.

"Purpose of your visit?"

"Graduate school."

"How long do you intend to stay?"

"Two years."

"Are you here by yourself?"

That question stung but I recovered quickly.

"Yes."

"Welcome to America," he said with a smile, handing the stamped passport back.

I collected my bags from baggage claim and was loading them onto a cart, when an officer with a dog approached.

As the dog sniffed my bags, he asked, "what eatables are you carrying?"

"Rice and snacks."

"Is the rice uncooked?"

"Yes."

"Tell me about the snacks."

"Sweets and munchies."

"Why are you insulting me like that? Tell me their names. Gulab Jamun? Pedha? Murukku?"

I told him the names.

"If I opened your bag, will I find expensive dresses or saris or jewelry?

"No sir."

"Have a good trip."

At the exit, I handed my customs declaration form to another officer.

"You indicate you are carrying more than $10,000. Is that a check for your school?"

"Yes sir."

"How much cash are you traveling with?"

"$200."

"OK, you're good to go."

***

Ashish's friends, whose recommendation landed me in this program, came to the airport to pick me up. I couldn't tell if they were big guys or if my feeling diminutive made them look that way. They loaded my bags into their SUV, and we were quickly on our way. I lived with them for a few days and then moved into an off-campus apartment with roommates I met via a meetup organized by the university's informal Indian student body. Three of us in a three bed two bath. Ojas Sarin, Vedant Dalal, and KK. We walked together into a leasing office, put in the deposit and walked out with a signed lease. The living arrangement might as well have been a thatched hut for all I cared.

The idea was to knock the two years out, earn some money during the practical training to pay back debt, and get out. Somewhere in this timeline was a wedding ceremony that included family and friends. And then, when all the dust settled, run my own practice to design greener buildings in India. Meanwhile, Mira would be done with her own education to become a full-fledged fashion designer. All I had to do was hang in there and let things default to stability. In the end, there would not be any worries about money, love, and an ordinary life.

The first few weeks in America, anything but ordinary, were revelatory. The term adjustment would be an understatement. And jet lag didn't make things any easier. I used regular dish detergent when I loaded the dishwasher and the suds filled up half the kitchen. The ingredients on peanut butter did not contain dairy. We bought butter that contained no dairy. We bought milk in gallon jugs, not in half liter plastic pouches. Internet was a luxury before but now it was available round the clock. Hot water being always on was a novelty but hot water at kitchen sinks and bathroom faucets was unheard of. Traffic flowed in the opposite direction, at speeds unimaginable on Indian roads, even in the quaint college town of Scottsdale. Oh, and did I mention movie rentals at Blockbuster? Three discs at a time, as many as you could watch. Not that we had the time, but I had to get Jerry Maguire and Point Break out of the way soon.

"Have you watched the two movies yet?" I inquired on one of my weekend calls with Mira.

"Not yet, but I have started reading the novel."

"Oh, you must watch the movies. What do you think about the book?"

"I have never read anything like it. The lustful parts make it very difficult, especially with you being so far away."

"Tell me more," I chuckled.

"I can't. Not over the phone."

"Can we not play husband and wife for a moment?"

"Hold your horses, hubby. Good things come to those who wait."

Ah, waiting. I was twisting like a pretzel. I had to digress quickly.

"OK, how do you like the new school and fashion designing?"

"IIFD is all right. We have a course on sustainable fashion design that makes me think of you. We talk about materials, supply chains, child labor, and all that. I'm not enjoying the hazing part. Everyone drinks and smokes. Sometimes, I can't even tell what they're smoking. The hook up culture in Delhi is a big change compared to Lucknow."

"Let me know if someone messes with you too much and I will swoop in."

"And what will you do when you swoop in?"

"I've been told I'm good at breaking jaws," I chuckled.

"You don't get to do any of that. I will survive. An American cop will not look the other way like the Indian cop did."

"Understood. I must hang up now; I'm using up all the minutes."

"OK. It's still morning for you but it's getting past bedtime for me."

"The time difference is a killer," I concurred.

I must tell you about calling cards. We have a landline now. Calls to anywhere within the US are included but who needs that? International calling meant buying calling cards from gas stations and convenience stores that came with a set number of minutes for every $5 or $10 you paid. The rub was you had to watch the minutes very closely. A call that lasted three minutes and two seconds meant four minutes deducted from your balance. That felt brutal, but we did not have a choice.

The three of us had our own bicycles but I never imagined that I would buy two bicycles on the same day. The wheels of the first one I had secured to the designated rack with a cable lock in the morning were gone by the afternoon. And it was cheaper to get a new bicycle compared to getting the bad one fixed.

The American education system was also novel, based on semesters and not full years. We were graded on periodic assignments, tests, and active participation, and not on one-time year-end exams. We shared a computer lab at the university with other students but needed our own laptops for keeping up with student assignments at home.

Living with Piyush in Delhi did get me out of my shell, but the American living situation was Delhi on steroids, just like everything else. Ojas was an American citizen and a business student. And he was a hustler. He would be gone most of the time working odd part time jobs like gas stations and convenience stores. When he was around, he was good at doing his part with cooking, cleaning, and keeping the house in order. Vedant, the IT student, on the other hand was very irreverent. He missed his cooking turns and used other people's stuff without permission. Neighbors even complained to the management about the loud music blasting from his speakers. I had to apologize on his behalf because he was too smug to do it himself. Luckily, the Korean family did not escalate the issue further.

Another door down from the Korean family was a woman with a dog. She would walk her dog in the neighborhood, sometimes with an elderly lady, and sometimes by herself. I crossed paths with her one day in the courtyard of the apartment complex.

"Nice dog. I haven't seen one like yours before," I muttered.

"Thank you, her name is Asha. She is a Belgian Malinois."

"Oh, that is my mom's name too."

"What are the chances?"

"Can I pet Asha?"

"No, please don't do that."

"Not today or not ever?"

"She is not the friendliest dog there is. She is a rescue and does not like strangers."

"Got it."

"I'm KK by the way, it's nice to meet you," I said extending my hand.

"Yatzil," she replied, shaking my hand.

Yatzil's handshake was firm with a palm that didn't feel very feminine. I could sense calluses, probably from lifting weights. She had curly brown hair, a pale complexion and a slender build. She smiled gracefully and walked with an erect posture. I couldn't quite place her accent.

"I see you toiling away in the fitness center," I remarked.

"I see you running too. I don't know how you do it in this heat," she countered.

"I'm still getting used to air conditioning," I chuckled.

"Yeah? Once you get used to it, there is no going back. My mom doesn't have air conditioning in Mexico, but she runs it on full blast when she visits here."

The accent must be Mexican then, I thought to myself.

***

Grocery runs were more frequent because the quantities were limited by what we could bring back on bicycles in plastic bags. We avoided eggs because they would easily break in transit. Milk and cereal were the go-to breakfast. Ojas preferred toast with peanut butter. Vedant survived on coffee. I liked the convenience of canned goods because it meant less preparation. And thanks to Piyush, I could now pass for an amateur chef. Days turned into weeks, and summer wasn't showing any signs of letting up. The National Weather Service had issued an extreme heat advisory, which meant no outdoor activity unless necessary that September morning. We had assignments to complete, but classes were canceled.

I could hear Asha's muffled barking.

Ojas and I were prepping food in the kitchen. Vedant was watching TV in the living room.

"Turn up the exhaust hood guys, the sauté smell is too strong," Vedant yelled.

"Why don't you lend a hand?" I snapped.

"I have to leave shortly, and lunch is not going to fix itself," Ojas added.

We were beginning to give up on expecting Vedant to help with anything.

"It's the first anniversary of 9/11 guys; you can't miss this stuff on TV," Vedant yelled back.

A chill ran through my spine. The knife fell from my hand, bounced off the cutting board, onto the floor. A day of monumental loss in American history. But it was more visceral for me because it reminded me of how Piyush was brutally attacked a year ago. I had a sudden urge to check on Piyush. I walked toward the phone.

"Are you OK? Where are you going?" Ojas demanded.

"I need to make a phone call."

"Can we not finish up in the kitchen first?"

"I need to call India. It's already late evening there."

"Keep it brief, I can't do it alone."

As I reached for the receiver, I heard a faint thud. The lights turned off and the exhaust hum stopped.

"Did we just lose power?"

"Yes, the TV's out," Vedant said.

"So is the cook top," Ojas chimed.

There was enough light from the living room window but within a few minutes the apartment started overheating. We opened the main door and living room window to let the heat out.

Within an hour, it felt like we were going to melt. I wet a few towels, wrung the water out, and passed the extra ones around before draping one over myself. Exhaustion was beginning to set in.

"Hey guys, how is everyone doing?" said the voice of a silhouette that walked in through the door.

I could only see work boots, jeans and a brown jacket. If this was a maintenance guy, I wondered why his speech was slurred.

"What's going on?" I yelled through the towel covering my head.

"I have a gun and I need all the laptops and cash. No sudden moves. Everything will be OK," the silhouette replied. The voice sounded scratchier this time.

This can't be happening. Life has come full circle. The towels were not doing anything to help anymore.

"Stand back, you don't need to be a hero," said a faint voice in my head. Maybe a heat stroke was beginning to set in.

"Walk around and get what you need man," I yelled.

"You get up slowly, pick everything up, and bring it to me. Don't do anything stupid," the silhouette yelled back.

"Just give him what he needs," whispered Vedant, hunched over on the couch.

Ojas didn't even step out of the kitchen.

I got up with my arms raised and looked at him. There were no facial features under the baseball cap. Just a blank shadow. There was a pistol in his right hand.

I unplugged the chargers and wrapped the power cords around the laptops. The phone was only feet away on the end table by the couch, but this time I was going to comply. I stacked the laptops on top of each other and walked toward the intruder.

As I extended my arms to hand the laptops over, I heard a metallic thump. The intruder's head hit the arm of the couch and then the floor. That's when I saw Yatzil at the door with a baseball bat.

"Anyone want a chilled beer?" she said with a smile.

***

"I put off getting a driver's license too long, can't deal with this heat anymore," Ojas said, with a renewed sense of urgency. "I'm going to get a learner's permit today; does anyone want to go along?"

"Not me," Vedant replied.

"Me neither," I chirped.

"I wouldn't trust Vedant with a car. But KK, what about you? Don't you want to impress future clients with a flashy car? Or maybe take your future wife out for a nice ride?"

My breath escaped me for a moment. My voice quivered.

"Now that you put it that way," I faked a smile. "I haven't prepared for the written test though."

"I have the booklet and you can review on the way, it's easy!"

In a couple of hours, we were in line to pay the fee for a written test. I was fourth or fifth from the counter when a gentleman was turned away for not having an acceptable method of payment. I looked behind me and there were twenty people.

"By the time I go to the ATM and come back, the line will get even longer," I could hear him arguing with the clerk, to no avail.

"Excuse me, how much cash do you need, sir?"

"$20."

"I can loan you $20 and you can mail a check to me later at my school address."

"Are you sure?" he said, staring in disbelief.

"You seem like a nice guy. And you will be wasting half a day."

"I didn't think such things happened. Please don't let others take advantage of you."

I handed him a $20 bill and scribbled my address on a piece of paper for when he finished the transaction.

He waved on his way out.

"I can't believe you did that. What if he doesn't pay back?" Ojas asked, with a puzzled look.

"That's on him. I did my part."

Both of us took the test and passed it.

"What now?" I asked Ojas.

"Now you can legally get in a car to learn how to drive. We can enroll in a class together. Then we should come back to take the driving test. And then we get a proper license."

"Thanks for pushing me to do this."

"Of course."

"I have two things to tell you," I told Mira over the phone that night.

"One, if you can believe it, I have a learner's permit for driving a car now."

"I'm trying to visualize you in a car, but I can't get past the Vespa image," Mira chuckled.

"Look at the upside, you don't have to wear a poncho when it rains this time," I countered.

"I finally watched the movies you got for me at the train station. One of them was OK but the other one worries me a little bit."

"Tell me more," I urged.

"A guy jumping off a plane without a parachute? Another guy riding his surfboard into a fierce storm?"

"Aren't you taking fiction too literally?"

"I do worry about you. I worry about us. Remember, your returning in one piece is non-negotiable. What was the second thing you wanted to tell me?"

"Oh, it escapes me," I punted, struggling to bring up the intruder or Yatzil's rescue.

"Make sure to remember and tell me next time, it's getting late anyway."

The next day, the first paycheck from Prof, Cook's research assistantship arrived. Rent was getting split three ways. The principal on the student loan was intact, but the interest was only $100 a month for the next two years before heavier principal repayments kicked in. Things suddenly felt much lighter. Maybe owning a car doesn't have to be a luxury. I could get something basic, fuel efficient, and low maintenance. As a bonus, I could make scrambled eggs for breakfast. I enrolled in driving lessons and got my license soon after.

I mentioned to Yatzil during one of our sidewalk run-ins that I was looking for a basic but reliable used car.

"Moving up the ladder, are we?" she taunted. "I have a friend who works at the local car dealership. Maybe he can help you pick something that is not a lemon."

The car salesman started with "to make a long story short" and went on to explain how Japanese engineering ensured cars would last until you got bored of them and how a Honda or a Toyota was the right fit for me. We walked out with a Honda Civic.

"Did you know Arizona has all the weather patterns of the country in one state? Sedona is very scenic and if you're lucky, you might be able to catch some snow in Tucson. Winter break is coming up, and it can get very interesting for you if you plan ahead," advised Yatzil on the way back.

"I did not think about that but it sounds very interesting."

"We can map your road trip out over coffee if you want to come in for a minute," she offered.

I gratefully agreed.

The door opened and Asha went stir crazy as I walked in.

"Don't freeze up, close the door behind you," Yatzil chuckled.

"Can we do this at my place, please?"

"You must be patient with Asha. Once she develops trust, she will put her life on the line to protect you."

"This is my mom Paloma by the way. Mom, this is KK."

I smiled and waved.

"Sit down, I will mark up a map for you roughly, but you can order a precise map from AAA. That will be more detailed."

"Sounds good. Thank you."

"What are you doing for winter break?" I inquired while she was working on the map.

"Not much. I will be driving to Nogales to drop mom off. From there, she will catch a bus to Guadalajara."

"There are buses that go from the US to Mexico?"

"Sorry, I should have mentioned. The city Nogales is both in Arizona and in Mexico. I will be crossing the border to drop her off in Nogales, Mexico."

"That sounds scenic based on what you described earlier."

"It sure is. And it's only a few hours each way. That is why we do the drive every time. Now that I think about it, if you end up with no other plans, you could drive us there and put some highway miles under your belt. I will pay for the gas of course and offer you some driving tips on the way. Think about it, no pressure."

Paloma said something to Yatzil in Spanish that I did not fully comprehend. My best guess from the tone was - Making him cross the border twice?

"It's a kind offer. Did I tell you that my first time getting on an airplane was to come to the US? I feel like I'm still settling in. I just need to think a little harder about if I want to add a third country to my resume this quickly."

CHAPTER 7: LINE CROSSED

Mira or not, Mexico felt like a nice to have, not a must have. I shelved the idea.

One of the first things I did when I got up was check my email. I didn't realize when this became a habit, but it made for a morning routine that was quite different from my previous life. There would be something from Mira once or twice a week. When there was not much to share, we traded electronic greeting cards. The physical mailbox usually contained notices from apartment management or utility bills along with unsolicited marketing mailers. When I reached school that December morning, there was a piece of nondescript mail sitting for me at my lab desk. The sender was Robert Christman.

The envelope contained a thank you card and a check for $20.

"Sorry for the delay. I misplaced your note with the address. I hope you're driving safely. - RC," the handwritten note on the thank you card said.

The following Saturday, I was at the bank to deposit the check. As I walked out the glass doors after the transaction, I saw someone familiar getting down from a car in the parking lot. As she took her sunglasses off, I felt vivid flashbacks from my college time in India, hazing rituals, and my dodging Piyush's questions about my past life over cocktails.

"Priya Mallela, as I live and breathe!" I yelled.

"KK, what are you doing here?" came an equally enthusiastic response.

"You tell me. Weren't you supposed to be in Chicago?"

"Oh my god, this is too much. Let me wrap up at the bank and we can go get a coffee or something to catch up."

We pulled up separately at the coffee shop across the street.

"And I thought you had moved to Delhi and found your dream job," she said, taking a sip from her latte.

"I thought I was doing all right in Delhi too. But it turns out, life had other plans."

"I wasn't expecting to see you here but now that I think about it, I'm not surprised you landed here. This is the land of Ayn Rand and objectivism you were so high on."

"A lot has been overridden since then. I remember your cautioning me about being too idealistic. You were much more practical for your age."

"Being too practical has its downsides too, I guess."

That remark seemed very honest but very unlike the Priya I knew. Don't get me wrong, she was still strikingly beautiful, but it was evident she aged considerably over the last two years. The dark streaks under her eyes, a chipped tooth, and a manicure that was past its prime.

"Well, you sound wiser. If you're not in a rush, I'd like to know more."

"Where do you want to start?" she asked.

"Our conversations revolved so much around changing the world. I know your getting married so quickly and traditionally broke a lot of hearts, mine included. But before you go into the details, I want to apologize for my crass ways of pursuing you despite your friend-zoning me."

"Oh, the glamor queen. There is no need to apologize. I could never make up my mind. So, I let my parents take the lead," Priya added.

"I'm listening."

"Initially everything was fine, but the guy changed colors as soon as we landed in Chicago."

"What do you mean?"

"I have lost myself. There is no give and take in the relationship. He thinks he knows what is good for me. My parents feel disrespected and struggle to communicate."

"I'm sorry to hear that. I hope work provides some distraction."

"I'm not allowed to legally work in the States. I'm on a dependent visa."

"You're financially dependent on your husband?"

"More so legally than financially. We moved to Phoenix recently. Dad sends me money, but I do my personal banking outside Phoenix."

"What next?"

"He wants kids, but I'm not convinced it is a good idea."

"That's tough. I don't know what else to say or do."

"Enough about me. What is going on with you?"

"Education. Debt. And learning not to pressure others into romance. You know, the usual," I replied.

"You've always been too modest for your intensity. I would be surprised if that idealism hasn't broken any hearts yet."

"All I'm allowed to say is it's complicated," I said, lowering my eyes.

***

Over a phone call, I came clean with Mira about the day-trip-to-Mexico idea with a neighbor. I found her calm response insightful. I knocked on Yatzil's door to check if Mira's suggestion could work.

"Hey, is the invitation to Mexico still open?"

"It sure is. Are you going?"

"I want to go. What if I stopped in Nogales on the US side of the border for lunch and you picked me up on your way back after Paloma catches her bus?"

"That right there is some serious lateral thinking, my friend!"

"Thanks. I'm looking forward to it."

"Bring your camera along, we can stop at some scenic spots for pictures."

And thus, two days before Christmas, we were off to Nogales. Asha was boarded at a dog sitting place the evening before. My raw driving skills were put to a good test.

"You should always stay in the right lane and switch to the left lane only for passing," Yatzil pointed.

"At a stop sign, you should stop like you mean it. A rolling stop can get you a ticket."

"If you hit someone from behind, no matter the reason, you will be at fault," she observed, as we drove past an accident scene.

"When you're turning right on a green signal, remember that pedestrians still have the right of way. Let them cross first and then turn."

My Sony Walkman came in handy with keeping conversation to a minimum on the way to Nogales when Yatzil was driving. I sat in the back and gave Paloma and Yatzil some space. We stopped at places like Tucson and El Charro Cafe.

At the restaurant in Nogales where I waited, when an hour's wait turned four, I began wondering if I needed to start looking for alternative transportation to Scottsdale. That's when Yatzil walked in looking tired.

"You're not going to believe it. The line of cars getting back into the US is always long, but they pulled me over for a secondary inspection," she said, adjusting her hair over her ears.

"What is a secondary inspection?"

"That's when they ask you more questions, inspect your car, etcetera. They took my papers and disappeared for three hours."

"Did they tell you why?"

"They say it's random, but who knows. Maybe they forgot I was in the lobby or maybe they were trying to crawl under my skin."

"How did it end?"

"When they brought me my papers back and told me I was in the clear, I asked what I could do to prevent something like this happening again."

"What was their response?"

"Just a shrug."

"All's well that ends well."

"I didn't want you to worry that a Mexican lady stole your car. Let's get back on the road now. We can stop on the way for dinner. And can you drive all the way this time? I'm too exhausted."

"You can take a nap if you want," I told Yatzil once we got on the highway.

"I'm too frazzled to drive or fall asleep."

"Can I ask you something personal?"

"Shoot. I will tell you if it's too personal."

"How is it that someone as eligible as you are single?"

"You're a straight shooter, aren't you?"

"We have almost three hours to kill, would you prefer to talk about something else?"

"No, that's fine. I got divorced earlier this year."

"I'm sorry to hear that. Was it an overbearing husband?"

"No. I cheated."

Nobody said anything for a few seconds.

"Anything else you want to know?"

"Thanks for telling me."

"Only two more hours left. Why don't you share something interesting about you?"

"I've never had a Margarita before."

"Let us check that box over dinner. I will drive afterwards."

***

The Nogales trip and Christmas festivities put a nice bow on the first semester. Vedant was in India and Ojas was hustling to earn some extra cash during the holidays. My research assistantship was also on a break for the holidays.

"What are your plans for the day?" Ojas inquired.

"Not much other than back-to-back movies from the rental place," I replied.

"Why don't you hang out with me at the convenience store? I need some help restocking the racks."

"I'm not good at that stuff."

"Just this one time? I have a dentist appointment, and you can man the store for just a couple of hours while I'm gone. The owner should return and relieve you. It will be over in a blink."

"Why didn't you tell me about this before?"

"I tried to reschedule the appointment, but they didn't have any openings for a month or so."

"I'm not allowed to work off campus."

"You're not getting paid. You're just doing a friend a favor. No one needs to know."

I fidgeted with the TV remote for a second.

"Still not sure. What if the owner does not return on time?"

"OK, let's plan on my relieving you. You can leave even if the owner is late."

"Ok then," I said, begrudgingly.

Once we got there, the door chimed every time it opened. Ojas showed me around the store. Snacks, soda, beer, ATM, and the register. We stacked the empty beer cooler racks with single serves, 6-packs, 12-packs, and 24-packs. There was only one 36-pack of Bud Light left, more stock was expected the next day. It took me a minute to learn how the register opened and closed for cash versus credit card transactions.

"Why is this baseball bat behind the register?" I asked.

"That's just for safety. I have never had to use it."

Ojas left around 4 p.m., reminding me how I will be out by 6 p.m., no matter what.

The crowd was on and off. Someone wanted beef jerky, someone else bought a few lottery tickets. A group of preteens walked in smiling and hovered around the candy and soda areas. I had to ask them to leave once I was convinced that they were not serious customers. I kept looking at the clock, but time was passing at its own rate.

Around 5:30, the door chimed, and in walked a guy in blue jeans, a black round neck t-shirt, and a black ball cap.

"How are you doing, man?" he said with a smile, as he walked toward the beer cooler in the back.

He walked back with the 36-pack Bud Light beer and set it on the counter. As I reached for the scanner, he picked the box back up and dashed out of the door.

I jumped over the counter and ran toward the side alley where he went. He was sitting in a car on the front passenger side with the window rolled down. He seemed shocked to realize I had followed him. I lunged through the window and grabbed his collar. The car took off and turned right on to the main street facing the store. Confused by the car movement, I left his collar and braced myself to the open window to avoid falling. The car gathered speed after turning.

"Punch him! Punch him!" yelled the driver of the getaway car.

I could see the sky. I was in a fetal position, hanging from the open window by my armpit, with my heels dragging on the road. I turned my head to the right and saw the wheel spinning, below my head.

The thief in the passenger seat tried to land blows on my face with a clenched fist but couldn't quite reach it.

He tried to roll the window up, but the glass poked my armpit and stopped short under the weight of my body.

"Let me go! Let me go!" I cried.

The car slowed down and I rolled off.

All this probably lasted 30 seconds. It felt much longer.

I walked back to the store in a daze, trying to digest what had just happened.

There was someone standing outside the store.

"I saw what happened. The store policy is to not chase anyone beyond the door. Let's check your arm," he said, ushering me inside.

I inferred he was the owner.

"Just some bruising, you will be fine. You might have to get new shoes, though," he observed. "Just sit down and catch your breath."

A car pulled up, directly in front of the store's main door with a screech and the owner rushed out.

The thief was back, this time with a gun.

"Does he know who I am? Does he know who I am?" he yelled relentlessly pacing back and forth. His initial shock from being chased seemed to have turned into rage.

"He is new. Today is his first day, he doesn't know the store policy," the owner urged, as he tried to physically block the thief from entering the store.

But the guy made it through, and the owner just stood there, staring in disbelief.

I was frozen in place, no reaction left in me.

The thief leaned over the counter, pressed the gun onto my abdomen, and I heard a bang. The last thing I remember was staring into his cold expressionless eyes.

***

"Why did he have to shoot him three times?"

"Load him onto the ambulance, quick! He has lost a lot of blood!"

"Gunshot wounds! Coming through!"

I was looking down at my own surgery from above the spotlight pointed at my abdomen.

"Hey guys, I'm not in there! I'm here!" I waved frantically to get the surgery team's attention, "you might as well stop what you're doing! it's not going to work!"

I lay down in my dad's arms. "I got you this time, my son! I won't let the world hurt you anymore! Everything will be fine from here on!"

"I know how you're feeling. We will work through this," Mira calmly reassured me.

"You keep falling from that bed, KK," Piyush whispered in my ear, while hugging me tightly.

Light felt like needle pricks on the eyes when I opened them.

"How long was I gone?"
"18 days."
"Where am I?"
"Arizona Trauma Center."
"Did anyone come for me?"
"I will have someone look into it."
I looked at my palm and didn't recognize it.
"You're a little undernourished and dehydrated right now but it will get better."

"Your emergency contact Yatzil Covarrubias was here a few times. She dropped off a laptop that we've kept charged. We've informed her that you're awake now," said the nurse.

"Can you look through my inbox for email messages from a Mira Chatterjee?" I implored the nurse.

"I'm afraid we can't do that for privacy reasons, but I will check with our legal team about how we can help you. Maybe Yatzil can help you with it. Or you can wait a few days until you're able to sit up."

Eventually, I would learn that the shooting incident was widely reported in local and international news. The Indian Embassy in Phoenix got involved and were closely monitoring my case for financial and legal help. Mira sent me several emails daily until they stopped coming around the 10th day. They were painful to read. Besides expressing how much she loved me and asking if I was seeing the emails, she informed me that my dad had passed away from a heart attack a couple of days after the news broke. And that the news media in India highlighted me as a cautionary tale more than a victim. Some reports went so far as to suggest that I was using a student visa to work, at least until Ojas' clarification to the media about what happened on that fateful day began to dispel that myth.

I hit the 'reply' icon on Mira's last email and typed, "I survived the shooting. Still recovering. I have a lot to share."

There was an instantaneous auto response stating that the recipient's email address could not be reached.

PART 2 - LAWFUL PRESENCE

CHAPTER 8: THE BODY NEVER FORGETS

"Scans show blunt force trauma to your knees," said a nurse I had never seen before. She was dressed in all black unlike the other ones.

"Why are they blue? Did they use the reflex hammer too hard?" Dad said, running his palm on my knees.

Mom's saree was wrapped high around her neck, was it hiding gilt jewelry or the lack of any jewelry?

I drifted in and out of consciousness.

My mouth felt parched when I woke up. I lifted the sheets to check my knees, but the hospital gown covered them fully.

I looked at the page-a-day calendar on the nightstand. Dad's funeral happened two weeks ago.

"Were my knees injured when I arrived here?" I urged the nurse who walked in with a tray of food.

"Nothing is wrong with your knees. Maybe you're feeling anxious about getting up and moving again. Your abdominal sutures on the other hand are healing well. How is the pain medication holding up?"

"It's fine."

"Yatzil is waiting for you in the lobby with a gentleman, do you want them to visit now or after finishing lunch?"

"Now is fine."

***

Yatzil walked in with a quiet smile; I could hear her moist eyes asking: what did you do to yourself? The gentleman who walked in with her was bald, sporting a mustache and thick glasses. His pudgy fingers were holding a file.

Yatzil put her hand on mine gently and said, "How is the recovery going?"

"It's going all right. Where is the baseball bat?"

"Tucked away, to be employed again at the right time," she chuckled.

"I have to tell you everything that happened."

"There is plenty of time to talk about that. Meet Mr. Cooper, he is an administrative counselor from the university. He wants to talk to you."

"Hello, Mr. Cooper."

"Hey KK. I want to give you an update on what is going on with your academic situation. The university, along with law enforcement, immigration authorities, and the Indian embassy are in the process of conducting a thorough administrative review of the developments. Some case information and forms you should be filling out are in this file I will leave behind. Regardless of the outcome, one of the therapists from the university will engage with you to help you cope with any residual trauma. Do you have any questions for me?"

"What kind of therapy?"

"Just some conversation. Nothing too demanding."

"I don't know if that is necessary."

"It is not required but I think it will help your review process to demonstrate that you're doing your part. You can choose to discontinue anytime."

"OK."

"The file also has my business card, just in case any questions come up as you're going through the file."

"What happens when I return to the classroom?"

"You have some catching up to do, but it should be business as usual unless you're told otherwise."

Mr. Cooper left.

"Do you need an update on the guy that shot you?" Yatzil asked.

"Not particularly," I said. "I don't blame him."

"OK, on the apartment front, your roommates vacated and disappeared."

"What? Just like that?"

"Yup. Do you want to keep paying rent for a three-bedroom apartment?"

"That will get too expensive."

"I can put you on my lease for now, until you figure out what comes next. Think about it."

"Will do. That is kind of you."

"Now do you want to tell me what happened?"

"Did you see what's in the file?"

"That information is for you. We will have plenty of time to do a scene-by-scene enactment once you fully recover. I will leave this box of cookies on the table, make sure to check if you can eat them yet."

She bent over and gave me a peck on the cheek before leaving.

***

I was checking email when the screen abruptly refreshed. There it was, a message from the upside down.

My sutures burned like someone lit a matchstick to them.

"It's hurting!"

The nurse rushed in, connected the IV drip and injected a clear liquid into it.

Sender: Bina Chatterjee. Subject: Our plans for Mira
I don't know how long I stared at it before I opened the email.

KK, I don't know how you're doing or if you're using email yet. After you appeared in the media, Mira shared the news about the wedding and the need to visit you. Given the gravity of the situation, I had to break the news to my parents. In India, even a private wedding ceremony is legally binding, more so given the photograph. After a family huddle, we concluded that Mira would seek an annulment. I have attached the attorney's notice. If you're not fit enough to travel now, we can pick a date that works for you. Do acknowledge the receipt of this email. Peace. Bina.

The pain subsided. The screen blurred. A tear rolled down my cheek. I slid back under the covers.

***

The train will arrive on platform number 6, the announcement blared on the train station speakers. I checked the signage, but the platforms were not numbered. Mira was standing on the platform across the tracks, motionless. As I looked around, the tracks stretched far in both directions but there were no pedestrian bridges. I approached the edge of the platform to cross the tracks. And the ground shook.

"You mentioned bruxism under your medical history. Tell me more about your dreams," the therapist said, adjusting her glasses.

"The ones I remember, they are not easy to share."

"We can revisit that at another time then. How do you feel your recovery is progressing so far?"

"A week into classes, I feel it is heading in the right direction. I used to ride a bicycle earlier, and I got a car just before the shooting incident. So, that is helping."

"Are you able to focus in the classroom?"

"I feel like my focus has gotten better after the shooting."

"How so?"

"When the shooter walked in and pressed the gun onto my abdomen, I stared into the shooter's eyes for a moment before the gun went off. I somehow felt grounded in that second."

"Knowing danger was imminent?"

"Yes."

"And that grounding sensation has stayed with you after?"

"It's more of a refusing to fade than lingering."

"That is interesting," the therapist said, making notes.

"I have a question."

"Shoot."

"Everything I tell you here, is it between you and me?"

"It is confidential. I will only relay your overall progress to the administrative review, not any of the details you share here."

***

I have been to many homes that were functional because of women, but the one I had lived in was my own in Star City, where my mother held the fort. I noticed curated order in my landlord's home in Delhi, compared to our tenant situation. Yatzil's home felt even better.

Indoor plants, candles, oil diffusers, folded linens, groceries organized in the fridge, silverware sorted perfectly, I could keep going. Asha didn't feel threatened by me anymore but kept her distance. Yatzil was my first female roommate ever, and it was also my first time living with a dog. I made the guest bedroom my own niche.

That day Yatzil made tacos for dinner. It reminded me of the parathas Piyush made, only the stuffing was outside this time.

"These are yummy. You must teach me how to make them."

"Sure. And you must teach me a uniquely Indian recipe."

"We have a deal. That picture on the wall, is that your ex-husband in it?"

"Yeah, why?"

"Why do you still have it up there?"

"We're still friends and I honor the memory of the time I spent with him."

"That is confusing to me. I haven't met many divorced couples in India but the ones that do get divorced don't do such things."

She took her time to chew and continued.

"It works differently here."

"If you don't mind me asking, how did you immigrate to America?"

"I crossed the border without papers and then met Joe. We fell in love and got married. And I naturalized here because of the marriage."

"And the naturalization survived the divorce?"

"Once you're in, you're in."

I sipped on the water before going nuclear.

"What is your advice for someone considering a divorce?"

"I think you have to decide if love is conditional or unconditional."

"Please elaborate."

"Well, if it is conditional and the conditions no longer stand, you're out. And if it is unconditional, any issues that arise must be resolved, and love perseveres."

"How did Asha handle the separation?"

"Asha was Joe's dog. Joe took her away, but she became miserable. So, he brought her back. She chose me."

After dinner, I fired up the laptop and replied to Bina's email: "Why did Mira not send this notice herself?"

I popped the last pain pill for the day and fell asleep.

The next morning, Yatzil asked, "Do you know you grind your teeth while sleeping?"

"I will get a dental guard soon, I promise."

"You do not want to deal with a sleep-deprived Yatzil, trust me."

"I get it."

I walked over to the apartment I had previously lived in, two doors down. I peeked through the window and didn't see anyone. I tried the doorknob and the door cracked open. Crumpled napkins, empty water bottles, and plastic bags lay scattered on the carpet. The living room light was out. There was a plumber working in the bathroom.

"How can I help you?"

"I used to live here. Just passing by."

"The toilet is clogged. The folks who left here didn't take care of the place."

"I'm sorry, they ran away from me. I was hospitalized for a while."

"That's no excuse. Wait a minute, aren't you the guy who was shot in the convenience store?"

"I'm what remains. Do you need an autograph?"

I was working on an assignment that afternoon before the evening class. There was a knock on the door. I tried to get a view from the window but couldn't tell who was knocking. I knew Yatzil wouldn't. Asha was snoring. I went back to my assignment.

An hour later Joe walked in with Yatzil.

He came to a halt when he saw me.

"Who is this guy? It looks like you didn't waste any time."

"He is a friend. And how does it matter to you?"

"It does. My girl Asha lives here too. How long have you known this guy and why is he here?" Joe said, pointing his finger at me.

I stood up, lifted my shirt to show my abdomen, and quietly said, "I'm just a guest recovering from surgery, sir."

"Were you here when I knocked earlier?"

"Yes."

"Why didn't you open the door?"

"It's not my house, sir."

Asha went stir crazy.

Joe scratched his head.

Asha approached me, sat down next to me, and started licking my feet.

Joe walked out.

Asha turned on her back with her belly and legs pointed toward me.

"Give her a nice belly rub, she is submitting to you," Yatzil instructed.

"Just when I thought I repulsed all girls equally!" I chuckled, as I complied.

***

"Welcome in, have a seat. How are you?"

"I'm doing OK, thanks for asking. How about yourself?" I replied, sitting down.

"Great! Just clearing the previous session from my head in time for yours."

"Is it a more complicated situation than mine?"

"Just different."

"I wanted to share something today."

"Let's start with that."

"I remembered trying to seek help before."

"In what sense?"

"When my love was not reciprocated in the past, I struggled with it. And I asked my mother to take me to a mental health clinic we would pass by sometimes."

"And?"

"By the time she agreed, I changed my mind. I needed it but wasn't convinced we could afford it."

"Thanks for sharing that. Has that unreciprocated love situation resolved with the passage of time?"

"Very recently, when I was least expecting it. Or maybe it has been eclipsed by bigger issues now."

"OK. I have a question for you now."

"Ask away."

"Is there a reason you went to your mom and not your dad?"

"I didn't think my father would understand."

"Why so?"

"He was either inebriated or absent."

"How about your mom?"

"She was the ballast."

"Hmm," the therapist said, and scribbled on her notepad.

"Has your father's alcoholism gotten better with time?"

"It consumed him. He died recently."

"I'm sorry to hear that. That must have been hard."

"It is what it is. I was in an induced coma when it happened."

"Any other relationships you want to talk about? Siblings? Significant others?"

I turned my head toward the window, but the blinds were closed.

"What if I can't be honest and I can't lie?"

"That's a predicament. Let's pick it up in the next therapy session."

***

We had a field trip planned at school that day. We were going to visit some built examples of buildings with downdraft cooling towers that used mist to cool air intake through evaporation. I had hinted to Prof. Cook that I may not be able to keep up with the others all day.

"Just stay in the bus when you need to catch your breath or find a cool spot and sit there. We will take plenty of pictures for you."

I was still working in the lab. Through the window, I saw the bus pull up in the driveway downstairs, ahead of time.

Bina's email response landed: We're protecting her. The media has moved on, but she is too distraught. Thanks for acknowledging the receipt of the attorney notice. Have you thought of dates for your visit?

I replied: How do I know she wants this annulment? Does she even know that you all sent me this notice? You both may share the same soul, but Mira and I are husband and wife now.

Bina responded quickly: Do you realize a judge can choose to grant an annulment in your absence if you're a no show? We now have evidence that you received the notice and are being argumentative. Just give us a good date for appearing at the hearing in person.

My ears started ringing. I closed the laptop and walked toward the bus early. By Indian standards this was a luxury bus with tinted glass and air that was too cold for comfort.

The bus driver seemed to be bobbing at music on the radio.

"Hello," I said, as I walked in.

No response.

I sat down in the first row, right behind him.

"Is that The Doors? I like them too!"

No response.

I assumed he couldn't hear me or didn't want to be bothered. At least the music was good.

"Why do you guys come here?" he muttered, lowering the music.

I was still alone on the bus with him.

"Pardon me?"

"Do they not have universities in India or wherever you're from?"

"Opportunity."

"What if I wanted to go drive a bus in India right now, will they let me do that?"

"I'm not here to work."

"That's what everyone says but they stay anyway."

"Listen, man. I'm already having a bad day; can we just tone it down a little? Others will be here any minute."

"Do you think I'm scared?"

"Well, aren't we paying for your job in a way? Shouldn't you be feeling thankful?"

"People like you come here and bomb our buildings or take our jobs. You should just go back to where you came from."

I was having trouble putting words together into a sentence. I took a deep breath.

"What is your name, man?"

"Let's say it is Harvey. Why, are you going to report me? That doesn't scare me."

"Have you heard of Taekwondo, man?" I inquired.

"Yes, are you an expert?"

"I'm an amateur but there are five tenets. Courtesy, Integrity, Perseverance, Self-control, and Indomitable Spirit. I think I am OK with four of them, but I don't know if I will ever be able to master self-control."

"So, you'll beat me up in a fit of rage? Have you looked at how scrawny you are?"

"No, but-"

Chatter erupted as other students walked into the bus. I got up, went and sat in the back row.

When we returned to the lab, I replied to Bina's latest email: I will be there in July. During the summer break.

***

I did not sleep a wink that night. My mind wandered.

Creation did not seem that benevolent anymore. Why would it put people with such different worldviews together in one situation?

Why were people like the shooter and the bus driver put in my path? I could see how engaging with the shooter violated store policy. But what about the bus driver? What does one do when the other person is violating a social policy?

Were mom and dad meant to be together? Or was it a cruel accident? Did dad drink because that was his only way out of debt? Did mom endure because that was only way out of a dysfunctional marriage? Could they have taught me something they didn't themselves master?

How did people like Piyush, Charlotte, and Yatzil make peace with the world? Or are they just good at living double lives?

I was a zombie at the dentist's place next morning. Nature photographs scrolled on the screen while I waited.

"No cavities yet but you will have to start using a guard. My assistant will help take the impression of your upper jaw using a mold." the dentist observed.

"How much will it cost?"

"My assistant will give you the options. The thicker ones are more expensive but will last you longer. That is what I would recommend for you."

"What if I can't afford it?"

"You can't afford not to. I'm surprised you are not experiencing sensitivity yet. Ask her about payment plans."

***

"Coffee?"

"Sure."

"Is there anything you want to talk about today?"

"A lot of things, time permitting."

"I'm looking at my notes. When we ended last time, you couldn't lie or be honest."

"Yeah, about that, do you think love is conditional or unconditional?"

"What do you think?"

"Unconditional."

"But what if your partner thought it was conditional?"

"I will meet the conditions."

"Even if doing that made you unhappy?"

I sipped on the coffee from the paper cup.

"In that case, I will negotiate."

"With yourself or with the other person?"

"Both."

"So, it's OK for love to be conditional sometimes then?"

"I'm confused."

"Ok, let's go back to your parents if you don't mind."

"What about them?"

"It seemed like love was unconditional for your mom and conditional for your dad. Is that a good characterization?"

"Yes."

"And they negotiated?"

"Yes, but miserably. They didn't know where to meet each other."

"You are onto something here. What do you think they should have done?"

"The most obvious option was to separate."

"Why do you think they didn't?"

"Social and financial pressures. Me."

"If we honored their choice of sticking together, how could they have negotiated with each other better?"

"Maybe mom could have been firmer with an ultimatum like quit alcohol or I will quit the marriage."

"But your mom doesn't seem like a fighter."

"Maybe dad could have been more sensitive to what made mom happier."

"In our next therapy session, let's talk about what you can do internally before you try to negotiate with the other person."

"Sounds good."

***

"Hey, what is your best strategy for international air tickets? Do you go to agents or get tickets online?"

"There are online options but if you need flexibility, an agent might be your best fit. Why, are you going to India for spring break?" Yatzil asked.

"For the summer break, not spring break," I said.

"When will you be gone?"

"All of summer break. June and July."

I hadn't admitted it to myself yet, but my plan was for scheduling the court hearing in July, so I can go ahead of time to confront Mira and maybe change her mind.

"What about spring break then?" Yatzil inquired.

"I don't have anything planned. I remember an old friend recommending the Grand Canyon."

"An awesome hiking opportunity but with your in-progress recovery, a daytrip with Asha should work. What do you think?"

"Let's do it. Another question."

"Shoot."

"Why do people get credit cards? Why not just spend using one's debit card? The price of the product you buy doesn't change!" I wondered aloud.

Yatzil shrugged. "Well, you pay a small processing fee on every transaction, but you have a line of credit you can draw from in time of need. It's a kind of insurance."

"Ah," I said. "I'm so used to paying for everything upfront, I didn't think about that. You learn something new every day."

CHAPTER 9: CONDITIONAL LOVE

"The scale of the desert is breathtaking," I said, pointing out the window on the drive there. "I've ridden a camel in vast Indian deserts, but this is on another level."

When we got there, stillness of the rock formations confronted me. These rocks don't move; the elements move through them. Erosion and time make them more graceful.

"I wish I could let Asha run around here without a leash," Yatzil said. "Not my favorite park policy but we must comply."

"Will she not get lost in this vastness?"

"I'm certain she will come back. She always does."

We capped the visit with a view of the sunset from Hopi Point. The yellow and orange hues were a sight to behold. The textures on the ground seemed reflected by the clouds in the sky.

"You saw the winding roads, are you comfortable driving in the dark?" Yatzil asked.

"Yes."

And so began the drive back.

"Hey, I have a question," I said, adjusting the rearview mirror.

"What's up?"

"What is the point of no return for a couple – when a marriage has to end?"

"I don't know. Every couple is different."

"We have four hours to kill. I don't mind some context on how yours happened."

"Broken marriages are a buzzkill. Are you sure that's how you want to spend the drive?"

"It's dark outside. We're not going to miss anything scenic."

"You asked for it. Joe was fine when we first met. But drug abuse and anger issues surfaced later. He used up his share of our money and hid the fact that he misused my share. At his peak, he cracked the computer screen open with a scissor. I felt extremely lonely and isolated. I ended up cheating to fill the void."

"Did you consider couples therapy?"

"We had appointments lined up but he would either cancel last minute or end up being a no show."

"Did you attend the sessions?"

"A few, but what's the use? I had my own issues, but I couldn't force him to go."

"Do you think he would have been comfortable going by himself?"

"Tried that too, didn't work."

"Whose decision was the divorce?"

"Mine. I served him when I disclosed that I cheated."

"How did he take it?"

"Not well, but what could he do?"

"So, what's your takeaway from all this?"

Red and blue lights lit up the road and the rearview mirror.

"Pull over to the side when you're able to. Provide any documents requested but you can decline to answer all questions."

"What?"

"I'm here, but you're the driver."

I pulled over to the shoulder. I lowered the driver's side window.

"License and registration, please."

I complied.

"Where are you coming from?" the cop asked, checking the documents with a flashlight.

"Grand Canyon."

"Where are you headed?"

"Scottsdale."

"Do you know why I pulled you over?"

"No."

"And who's that in the passenger seat?"

"My friend."

"Hands on the steering wheel, where I can see them. I'll be right back," the cop said, and walked back to his car. He came back in a few minutes.

"I need your ID, ma'am."

"I'm a passenger, I don't need to provide an ID."

"You do, when I ask for it."

"Do you suspect me of a crime?"

"Both of you get out of the car, please! And no sudden moves. Keep the dog close to you."

"Did you work in violation of your visa rules, Mr. Sharma?" the cop asked, patting me down.

Asha seemed visibly nervous when Yatzil got a pat down. I had to restrain her between my legs.

"No, officer."

"Why were you at the store that day?"

"To help a friend."

"Is that the answer you're sticking to?"

"Yes, officer."

"Why're you traveling with Mr. Sharma today?" the cop asked, turning to Yatzil.

"I don't answer questions," Yatzil replied.

The red and blue light was harsh. I was already surprised by Yatzil's responses but now, my knees felt weak.

"Do you consent to your car being searched, Mr. Sharma?" the cop asked, turning his attention to me.

"That violates our rights, officer," Yatzil countered.

"I thought you were just a passenger. I'm speaking to Mr. Sharma here," the cop shot back.

"OK," I muttered.

He turned the car inside out and walked back to us.

"I found this in your glove compartment, care to explain?" he asked, pointing to a tiny glass bottle with a transparent sticker that read 'opium.'

"It's gas station deodorant, officer."

"I didn't know they made deodorants with that name. Why are you carrying deodorant in your glove compartment?"

"It's a road trip through a desert, officer."

"I'll have to send this to the lab for testing," the cop said, wrapping the bottle in an evidence bag.

"Are we free to go?" Yatzil inquired.

"Drive safely."

My breathing eventually became less rapid. GPS indicated we had an hour left.

"Relationship with yourself comes before relationships with others," Yatzil said, almost whispering.

"What?"

"You asked for a takeaway from the divorce."

***

"How did spring break go?"

"Very well. Grand Canyon was beautiful."

"You should do something similar but longer for the summer break."

"I wish."

"Anything specific you want to talk about today?"

"I can't think of much."

"My notes indicate we stopped at what your mom and dad could have done better to meet each other halfway."

"Yes."

"How did your dad talk about his past, about this youth?"

"Heroic descriptions about exercising well, standing up to the system frequently, being very independent, and the like."

"How did he reference his time about being a husband before becoming a father?"

"Nothing much changed."

"Did he ever talk about collective decision-making or making space for your mom in his thinking?"

"No. He complained that she never listened."

"How was his relationship with you? Did you feel heard or accounted for by your father?"

"Not really."

"Why do you think he took to drinking?"

"I think the pressure of family life and financial burden got to him."

"Would you agree that he didn't give you and your mother enough weight in his thoughts or actions?"

"Yes."

"Did you think about what would happen to your family before chasing the shooter?"

"I wasn't expecting the guy to run with the beer. It all happened too fast."

"That's fair. Now give me an example of how consideration for someone close to you impacted your decision-making."

I couldn't explain how I complied with the intruder during the break in because I wasn't ready to talk about Mira. I explained the DMV encounter where I loaned $20 to a stranger.

"Hmm," the therapist said, making notes.

✦❋✦

"It's OK to wait for Mira but I hope you haven't stopped having fun," Piyush said, chuckling over the phone.

"There are plenty of pretty girls in Arizona, Piyush!" I countered.

"Anyone as pretty as Mira?"

"Maybe. I have a roommate who is smart."

"You didn't waste any time, did you?"

"She is just a friend."

"You haven't called once in almost a year, what's going on?"

"I need you to do some sleuthing for me."

"Tell me."

"Mira moved to Delhi for graduate school. But I don't know where she lives. Can you task someone with finding out?"

"Why don't you ask her directly?"

Such a mild reaction. Thank goodness Piyush didn't know Mira and I got married. He would blow a gasket if he found out.

"I want to send her a surprise gift."

"Can you tell me the names of the parents and where they work?"

I told him what I knew.

"Any suggestions on where I can begin?"

"She goes to IIFD's graduate program in fashion design. Maybe you can follow her home on a weekday."

"I can't afford to get beaten up again!" Piyush chuckled.

"I know you are joking but make sure there is zero direct contact," I cautioned.

It occurred to me that after the incident with Shanti and his brother, I hadn't checked on Venkat. He can be a bit aloof, tending to forget to keep in touch with people who help him.

"What's happening, Venkat?"

"Nothing earth shattering. I still owe you for help with Shanti."

"Not at all. I hope you're ready to graduate and start making some good money."

"Yes, I'm interviewing at a few places in Star City. The offers aren't bad at all."

"Are there any lingering issues with unrequited love?"

"I don't think the issues are going anywhere. I'm hoping to make peace with them by the time I start working."

"What about America? Your mom said you were very keen. I may have some pointers."

"Maybe for intermittent travel but I'm not looking to immigrate or anything."

"Project-based travel is the best thing. You get to experience the best of both worlds without unrealistic expectations."

"If I ever travel west for a project, you will be the first one to get a heads up."

"It will be great to spend time together again."

***

"Why is the parrot's beak missing?"

"I told you there were going to be challenges," the astrologer said.

"You told me I will be able to turn my life around but didn't tell me if Mira would work or how I would turn my life around."

"You will do very well in life."

"That's clearly a lie."

"Fate is not absolute. You can rewire things with effort."

"How convenient! I want a refund!"

"I neglected to tell you one more thing."

"What makes you think I'm interested?"

"I'll tell you anyway," the astrologer persisted. "You will have to choose between bringing your own child into the world and accepting someone else's."

"I didn't ask you tell me!"

"Now you know."

"Where does Mira figure in all this?" I yelled.

I woke myself up yelling. I reached for the water bottle on the nightstand. The clock read 3:14 a.m.

I unzipped the cabin bag's inner pouch and removed the envelope. I carefully pulled the wedding picture out of the envelope. I sat back on the bed and held it in front of me. That my mind was undecided about the wedding was clearly visible in my expression. I reached for the memory of that exact moment and could only think of exhaustion. Mira's look was that of relief, her smile as disarming as ever. The photograph was the only symbol of that rushed ritual, and the only thing missing in it was joy. I suddenly remembered my appointment with the family law attorney was that morning.

"Were you yelling in your sleep?" Yatzil asked at breakfast.

"The new dental guard is squeezing my jaw. I think it is also giving me nightmares," I replied.

"The next time you drag a bag out from under the bed, do it more quietly."

"Oh," I said. "That's embarrassing."

The law office was in a suburban office building with black tinted glass and crimson wall cladding.

"Coffee?"

"No, thanks."

"Did you bring the notice with you?" the attorney said, mixing creamer into his coffee.

"Here it is," I offered a printed copy.

"Ha!" he said, examining it.

"Is everything OK?"

"I'm just reading the justification for the petition. It says she regrets getting married in a rush and without family's approval. In America, they just cite irreconcilable differences; no justification required. The cultural difference is interesting."

"Anything else noteworthy?"

"They are asking for annulment because of non-consummation."

"What does that mean?"

"Invalidation of the marriage altogether, because you both haven't been intimate yet."

"Do you have anything stronger than coffee?"

"Well, I have a bottle of bourbon in the upper cabinet if you are serious," the attorney said, laughing. "Did the wedding get registered in the court?"

"No."

"So, nobody other than the two of you were at the wedding?"

"True."

"They are asking for the photograph back and are insisting you destroy all copies, print and electronic."

I took a deep breath. "What if I refused to attend the court proceedings?"

"It says here that the court can grant the annulment in your absence if you don't respond."

"What are my options?"

"You will have to hash that out with your Indian attorney. Different cultures, different laws."

"Any generic advice on strategy?"

"You may not like it."

"Lay it on me, please!"

"Women value emotional safety. If you figure out how to provide what Mira needs, maybe she will change her mind and defy family."

"How much do I owe you?"

"For this? nothing."

"I will put a gift card in the mail. Thanks."

***

The astrologer dream. The conversation with the attorney. My brain felt fried by the time the class on green building certification systems ended. I couldn't stop thinking about Bourbon. So, I paid a visit to the bar across the street from my school building.

"Bourbon and soda, please!" I said to the waitress.

"Single or double?"

"Make it a double. I'll be right back from the restroom."

As I walked out of the restroom, in the direction of my table, I felt someone crash into my shoulder. Before I realized, I was flat on the floor, staring at the ceiling.

"Look here guys, this is the guy who lives with my wife, and he even took her on a spring break trip," a familiar but slurry voice said.

It was Joe with two other guys.

"Ex-wife," I said, picking myself up.

"I stand corrected," Joe slurred, before landing a hard punch in my gut.

The sutures I thought had healed, now felt like a razor blade swipe.

I was standing but bent over now, holding my stomach in pain, looking at the floor.

The guy to my left raised his knee and landed a blunt blow on my face.

Blood dripped across my mouth onto my chin. Tears flowed down my cheeks. I momentarily blacked out.

When I came back it was all blurry. Through the corner of my eye, I saw the guy to my right swing his arm at my face. I stepped back and did an outer forearm block.

"Call 911!" I yelled at the bartender behind the counter.

I wiped my face with my sleeve.

I dodged another wild swing in my face.

"Listen guys! You all can keep hitting me, but I have something to say!"

"Yeah, what?"

"I shouldn't have corrected you, I'm sorry."

"A day late and a dollar short."

I quickly shifted and landed a targeted side kick with my right foot on Joe's chin with a loud roar.

Joe's head landed with a thud on the table next to him. The other two guys bolted out the door.

I slowly lowered my right foot from the air onto the floor in a circular motion.

Time stood still. I didn't want to move.

A seemingly elderly lady walked up to me slowly, held my arm and led me to the closest chair. She handed me a napkin.

"I'm Barbara, the owner of this bar."

"Hi, I'm KK," I said, wiping my mouth.

"You were brave out there. My son teaches Taekwondo and your side kick was very impressive."

"Thank you."

"As luck would have it, the only other customer in the bar got up and left as soon as the fight started. I had picked up the receiver to dial 911 but couldn't make up my mind."

That took a second to sink in. "Why?"

"You looked like an international student. We didn't want you to get dragged into any issues."

"I call bullshit on that."

There was a pause.

"OK, I will level with you."

"Please do."

"We have laws here that could lead to severe liabilities if they found out we served alcohol to already intoxicated individuals. Not to mention the harm to the reputation."

"It's making sense now."

"I can help clean you up. I'm offering you free drinks for lifetime. Just come over whenever you feel like it, there will be an open tab. Can we agree to forget this ever happened?"

"You guys have cameras here. I can call 911."

"How about I add $1,000 to sweeten the deal?"

I dabbed my nose with the napkin.

"$5,000 and we have a deal."

CHAPTER 10: THE COST OF SILENCE

After the bar fight, I went home late that night, showered, and went to bed. I hid the wad of cash in my cabin bag, next to the wedding photo.

The next morning, the phone rang when I was brushing my teeth. Yatzil picked it up and spoke for a minute.

"Hey, Joe wants to talk to you," Yatzil yelled.

I spat the foam out. There was a pink hue to it.

"What about?"

She spoke to him again and replied, "He wants to apologize for being rude to you when he came over the other day."

"I'll be a while. Tell him I accept the apology," I yelled back.

Classes continued. Therapy ended after two more sessions. During my last visit, the therapist told me that she would send her outcome report to the administrative reviewers dealing with my case. She wished me well.

My short stint in Delhi meant I lacked a useful network. I could turn to Nishkam, Ashish, or Piyush to help me find an attorney. Or I could represent myself. I kept putting the decision off, but the India visit was closing in.

Piyush would be subject to two heartbreaks —marriage and separation. Ashish was an avid networker. Ashish it was.

"Hey, thanks for taking my phone call."

"KK, you son of a gun!"

"I'm here in Arizona because of you, remember?"

"Nah man, it was all you. Can we do this quickly? We're heading out for dinner."

"OK, I need a good family law attorney with a practice in Delhi."

"Say no more. There's a trustworthy practice next door to Nishkam. I personally know someone who works there. I will email you the details."

I felt thankful no explanation was involved. Late that night for me, it was the next morning for the law practice. I dialed the number.

"Is this Attorney Viraj Mehta?"

"This is him. Are you calling from America?"

"Yes, from Scottsdale, Arizona. Ashish Damle sent me to you."

"How can I help you?"

I explained everything.

"Interesting," he said. "Forward all communications thus far to my email. Does a retainer of $1,000 work for you?"

My answer would have been different before the bar fight.

"Yes."

"I will send you the wiring instructions. All your communication from hereon will be through me. Do not, I repeat, do not engage with any communication that is not from me. If you receive something, you forward it to me. And you shut up. The time difference will be a challenge, but we will figure it out."

The next phone call a few days later was a bit more detailed.

"I have reviewed everything you sent me. What is your goal?" Viraj asked.

"To save the marriage," I replied.

"OK. I can investigate that possibility. So, when will you be in Delhi?"

"I haven't told you everything. It is a bit complicated."

"This is a good time to share."

"As far as Mira's attorney is concerned, I'm visiting in time for the hearing in July. But I will be there a month ahead of that to visit with Mira and change her mind."

"That's not going to work. All of us will have to be on the same page. I will float the idea of a hearing in July preceded by Mira and your meetings under attorney supervision in June. Let's see what they say."

"What about our privacy?"

"We can ask the other family members to stay out of it, but otherwise, either I'm in or I'm out. There is no middle ground."

"Oh," I said.

"How do you intend to ask her to stay?"

"I have no idea."

"Better get to it then. You have less than two months."

So, June for an out-of-court settlement effort, and if that failed, July for a court hearing. The timeline was now etched in my mind.

In the following weeks, I replayed several arguments in my head that would appeal to Mira as a wife and as a human being:

"If not for meeting your and Bina's expectations of higher education, I wouldn't be in America or half this mess."

"Our wedding photograph stays in my bag for safekeeping, but it is always close to my heart."

"Once we get together after our education, this will all be worth it, I promise. Our love will guide and protect us."

"We had an armed intruder in our apartment. I complied and didn't escalate because I was thinking about the both of us."

"I loaned $20 to a stranger that saved him half a day's time."

"I didn't know the store policy before chasing the thief. I had no idea he could turn into a gunman."

"My becoming an immigration cautionary tale in the media was a direct result of helping a roommate make time for his dental appointment."

"I lost my father and didn't even get to perform the last rites in the process of earning your love and trust."

"I attended therapy to become a better husband."

"I stayed calm when I got pulled over by the police for no reason."

"I spilled blood and unknowingly raised money for this negotiation."

"Let us shape our own destiny. Try to convince Bina and parents, and if they don't understand, leave them be."

***

Our capstone project for the second semester was designing an office building for a client. One exercise in the project was dedicated to balancing a 20% cost reduction due to economic headwinds. Either all green measures went away, leading to the project becoming minimally code compliant, or the project would find money to fund the green measures successfully. We all sent in our responses ahead of time, so Prof. Cook could bring them up on the screen in the class that day for a debate.

Student 1: We should always strive to do the right thing. The promise of green features should be kept and giving up is not an option.

Student 2: If we build cheap now, maintenance and renovation costs in the future will become burdensome.

Student 3: How much extra are we overpaying in utility bills if we cut the green measures completely? Shouldn't we be looking at capital expenditure and operating expenditure together?

Student 4: Have we factored in productivity increase and higher rents from green measures? A 2% increase in occupant productivity can pay for the entire project's budget.

KK: If all else fails, maybe we the owner can find efficiencies to trim the building size by 20% and keep the green measures.

Student 6: What was the basis for the original budget? Let us ask the owner to rewrite their requirements to list the top three non-negotiables and start from there.

Student 7: Aren't non-sustainable buildings becoming stranded assets, creating a liability in the longer term?

Student 8: Indoor environmental quality affects the health and output of the occupants. Shouldn't wellbeing be the driving factor in the decision-making process?

Student 9: Are we factoring in federal tax credits and other incentives fully before arriving at the 20% shortfall? Let us not leave free money on the table.

"Shouldn't the program inform the budget? Isn't it backwards for program to shrink and expand to accommodate market conditions?" Professor Cook grilled me, when it was my turn.

"I haven't finished debating that in my head, Prof. Cook," I said.

"Maybe the project can add a Phase II to expand later when a clearer solution emerges. What do you think?"

***

Late night phone calls were now a part of my lifestyle. I never felt like I got all the minutes out of the calling cards I was paying for.

"Piyush my friend, how are you doing?"

"All is well. What's happening?"

"I called to take back my request about sleuthing on Mira. I found the address."

"I didn't have the courage to follow a girl around the city anyway."

"OK."

"I did something better. I hired a PI."

"What is that?"

"A private investigator."

"Why?"

"Because I was waiting for you tell me about the wedding. And then you call to tell me you didn't know where Mira lived. That messed with my head."

"How did you find out about the wedding?"

"You didn't do a good job of hiding the photograph when you were packing for travel."

"Oh no! I told you zero direct contact."

"There wasn't any direct contact."

"Are you sure?"

"Affirmative," Piyush said. "I was going to call you about the findings. You beat me to it. Are you ready for it?"

"I don't feel ready for anything lately."

"Here they are, anyway. Mira's mother is fighting a cancer diagnosis. Bina has broken up with her boyfriend and is going through blackmail. And Mira is going through a divorce, which means you messed up big time."

"Oh boy," I said. "What has this world come to?"

"Are you ready for the zinger?"

"Let's find out."

"Mira's attorney is none other than Rakesh's father."

"What?"

"Believe it or not."

"I need another favor."

"You need a place to stay during your Delhi visit?"

"How did you know?"

"I'm negotiating job offers during a campus recruitment drive and will have my own apartment soon. I got you covered."

"What would I do without you?"

"Nothing, apparently! I will email you the details," Piyush chuckled.

The next phone call was to my Indian attorney.

"I'm glad you called," Viraj said. "I have a few updates."

"I'm listening."

"They have agreed to three mediated meetings between Mira and you. We will keep detailed notes."

"That's progress?"

"Now the bad news. They are not budging on the annulment. If no out-of-court settlement is reached, we default to the hearing in July."

"How long do you expect the court proceedings to last?"

"You will most likely need just one hearing."

"OK."

"Have you thought about what you will say to Mira?"

"Yes, but my strategy is evolving."

"Send me some notes when you get a chance."

"Anything else?"

"Lookout for an invoice for the next $1,000. Safe travels."

"Thanks."

***

Air travel to India was less anxious; it teetered on the edge of being fun. Yes, the situation with Mira was unresolved, but I wasn't by myself anymore—Piyush and Viraj had my back.

On the first flight we hit turbulence. Given the flight's long-distance nature, the attendants stuck to their commitments, and there was one turbulent moment where all bets were off. We held our food trays as if our life depended on it. One attendant got thrown off their feet and crashed with the food cart right after passing me and landed on the floor. My first instinct was to get up and help but the "please don't touch me sir" correction from almost a year ago was still fresh in my head.

On the second flight, the flight attendant recognized me from the news coverage.

"Immigrants are treated too harshly these days. We have an unused seat in the business class if you're interested," she offered.

Of course, I was traveling on important business. I took her up on the offer. I checked the first upgrade box.

"What would you like to drink?"

"Bourbon with soda, please."

"Single or double?"

"Double would be awesome!"

The crowded airports, the long immigration check in lines, the confusion about who needs to fill out which forms – India somehow functioned amidst the chaos. As I got my bags from baggage claim and headed to the exit, I was asked by folks dressed in plain clothes to step aside.

"Any expensive gifts?" one of them asked.

"Electronics, jewelry or perfumes?" the other one insisted.

They put my bags through the scanner again and as the bags emerged, they opened them and went through the contents one by one.

"What is in this envelope?" the first guy said.

"Just a photograph, officer."

"Why do all these clothes still have tags?"

"Some are gifts. Some, I will wear during this trip."

"What is in this pouch?" the second guy said. "Seems like cash."

They counted the cash. It was $4,300.

"Have you declared this?"

"No."

"Why not?"

"It's within the allowed limit."

"What are you going to do with it?"

"I don't discuss my personal life, sir."

"Wait here, it could be a while!" they said as they walked away with the cash.

They eventually came back with the bag.

"Here it is, you're free to leave."

"Can we have the cash counted again before I leave, sir?"

"What are you insinuating? It's all in there!"

"All I am asking is for a double check, sir. I know my rights."

"Let me take it back and get you a sealed bag with a certified machine printed label." The men disappeared again and returned with the promised package.

"What do I do if things are not as they should be?"

"The printed label has a case number and officer names. You can file a complaint."

"Welcome to India," read the sign above the exit door.

CHAPTER 11: MEDIATED MEETINGS

"Dude, this apartment is a huge upgrade, with all the guards, gates, and covered parking!" I said, as the cab pulled into a community with multiple high-rise buildings on stilts.

"I knew my post-MBA life was going to be an upgrade, but the world has certainly evolved while I was studying. And you know what the added benefit is? Nobody random can enter your apartment and beat you up," Piyush replied.

I walked past the entrance hallway and rolled the bags to one side of the living room.

"KK, meet Aditi. Aditi, meet KK," Piyush said, pointing to the girl sitting on the couch.

"You continue to surprise, Piyush!" I said, shaking Aditi's hand.

Conversation flowed. I dozed off on the couch soon after.

There was chatter that Mira was on her way. The other people in the room went about their business as if that was not of any consequence. I remained frozen in place, not knowing if leaving was better than staying. It was a reunion. Mira's and my classmates had no faces or names.

Jetlag was no less than hospital delirium at inducing nightmares. America refused to release me. India insisted it must prevail.

As the cab approached Viraj's office building, it passed Nishkam's place. I saw a small figure with her head down walking toward the door.

"Charlotte!' I yelled, lowering the window. "I can get out here," I told the cab driver.

"You've moved on from a Vespa to chauffeured services now?" she said.

"It's so good to see you! Have you given up your Canadian citizenship?"

"Likewise! Just backpacking and interning during the summer again," Charlotte replied.

"Did you bring Nishkam's coffee this time?"

"French Roast," Charlotte said. "Have you already said hi to Nishkam?"

"Not yet. I'm not sure I want to. Listen, I'm walking into an appointment, but would you have time for coffee in a couple of hours?"

"Let me check. Do you have a number you can be reached at?"

"I don't. I will just wait for you in that coffee shop across the street at 3 p.m. If you don't show up, I'll assume you're busy."

"That works."

"Welcome to our humble abode," Viraj said, picking me up from the reception area. "Our offices may be small, but we take pride in our work ethic."

The American attorney's office had central air-conditioning. Viraj's office had a wall mounted mini split. I wondered if Viraj kept alcohol in his cabinet.

"I've read your notes about how you intend to appeal to Mira. I'm sorry to say emotional appeals tend to fall short in these circumstances."

"That is all I've been thinking about. Jetlag hasn't been particularly helpful. Do you have any suggestions?"

"I know you came halfway across the planet to see her. You should make her feel seen," Viraj said.

It felt like Viraj was paraphrasing the American attorney's advice about providing emotional safety and winning Mira over.

"And ignore the attorneys in the room recording every action and every word?" I chuckled, unsure whether it was a joke anymore.

"If I left you to your own devices and Mira later said she felt threatened, would that be acceptable to you?"

"No."

"If they brainwash you into signing something in my absence, would that be acceptable to you?"

"No."

"That is the reality we are in. So, are you ready for your first mediated meeting coming up?"

"Where is it?"

"At Narayan Law Offices. Mira's attorneys."

"Why not a more neutral location?"

"I tried. Sorry."

"What is the name of Mira's attorney?"

"Rajesh Narayan."

"Anything else?"

"The accountant said we need to replenish your retainer."

I stared at the folder on the desk labeled KK vs Mira.

"Do you accept dollars?"

***

Charlotte was already there in the coffee shop when I walked in.

"Did you find something without chicory in it?" I inquired, sitting on a chair across from the table from her.

"Enough small talk. I saw the media coverage. Are you doing all right?"

"I deserved every bit of it. I didn't take your threat of a quiz on American culture before leaving seriously," I said, staring at the froth in my cup.

"Give yourself some grace. You are learning and growing like everyone else."

"The world always seems to be a few steps ahead of me."

"You can choose to exit the rat race and define your own place."

"If I tell you why that is a challenge, I'll have to kill you."

"Can I get a picture with you?" a stranger stopped and asked Charlotte. "My friend here will take it for me," he said, pointing to another guy with a camera.

"Sure," Charlotte replied.

The guy sat next to Charlotte, put his hand on her shoulder, and pulled her closer as the associate readied the camera for a shot.

Charlotte seemed confused.

"Honey, how many times have I told you not to engage with strangers?" I said, shifting next to her, moving his arm away, and putting my hand on her hand resting on the table.

"I never listen, do I?" Charlotte sighed, seemingly relieved.

The strangers with the camera walked away.

"See, you can tackle the world sometimes!" Charlotte smiled.

"I'm sorry, we should be treating tourists better."

"I've already forgotten about it," she said, waving her hand.

"I have a question for you," I said, circling the stirrer in a cup that was half full.

"What's on your mind?"

"Say, I was in a relationship with someone. How would I make them feel seen and provide emotional safety?"

"How many cups are we drinking today?"

"As many as we need to," I smiled.

"Listen more and speak less. Be respectful and transparent. Make eye contact. Non-verbal cues matter equally."

"How does a conflict shift that approach?"

"Continue to be respectful and validate where needed. Keep chipping away at the why behind the what."

"Charlotte, I want to marry you in another life!" I blurted.

"My ring size is 6."

***

Viraj and I walked into the conference room we were escorted to.

"Please be aware the cameras are on and are recording video and audio," the assistant cautioned.

Viraj set a glass of water in front of me on the table and stepped back. I had a full view of the large conference table and monitor mounted on the wall across it.

I stared at my own reflection in the monitor that was turned off.

The door creaked open and in walked a tall and overdressed gentleman with Mira closely following him.

I began to stand up when Viraj pressed my shoulder, forcing me back on the chair.

"Mr. Mehta, if everyone understands the terms, we can proceed with the meeting!" announced the person I assumed was Rajesh.

"Ready when you are, Mr. Narayan," Viraj replied.

Mira sat down across from me and pulled her chair forward. Her hands were on the table, one palm cupping the other. She wore the same sage green salwar kameez she wore during our second meeting. A bindi dotted the space between her eyebrows. Her eyes remained lowered, looking at her palms.

"My client chooses to remain present but silent today. We will still honor the one-hour commitment," Rajesh announced.

Viraj didn't say anything.

I observed her fingernails. Still as shapely as ever, but clipped in a rush. I took my copy of the wedding photograph out from the envelope and placed it in the middle. Inches away from her fingers, facing her.

I fixed my gaze on her eyes. She batted her eyelids more frequently. A tear rolled down her left cheek.

"You can start whenever you feel ready," Viraj whispered in my ear.

I took a deep breath, pushed the chair back with my legs, got up and started walking around the table, toward Mira.

"He can't do that!" Rajesh yelled.

"Mira can speak for herself," Viraj replied calmly.

Mira shifted in her seat.

I sat down in a chair next to Mira's. Our shoulders were an inch apart. I extended my right palm, lifted her palms into mine, and cupped them close with my left palm. Four palms stacked on each other.

I could hear Mira breathing. The next several minutes were the most conscious I had been of my own breathing. Our collective attention focused on the joined hands. I wondered if this was what meditation felt like. Seconds turned into minutes.

"Time's up!" announced Rajesh.

We slowly pulled our hands out, leaving behind a moist imprint on the glass countertop.

I got up, walked around, picked up the photograph, and carefully slid it back into the envelope.

"I've lost all hope for an out-of-court settlement!" Rajesh declared, running his fingers through his hair.

"I underestimated you," Viraj whispered in my ear.

"Next week, same day, same time!" Rajesh said, walking out.

I took a sip from the glass of water.

I felt such an overwhelming current in me that I had to hide in the restroom until I felt functional again. When I walked out, the assistant who showed us into the conference room earlier that day walked up to me.

"Did you forget you asked me to call a cab for you?"

"Oh," I said. "Sorry about that."

"The cab is waiting downstairs. I can walk you to it."

"Thanks."

"I can tell you are a very genuine human being stuck in the wrong circumstances," he continued.

"Where did that come from?"

"Just an observation. Because you're such a gentleman, I can relay some of our confidential details to you. They may not guarantee a certain outcome, but they will give you an advantage."

"I'm listening."

"And if you wanted me to look up any details from your history in our documentation and how we are using it, I can do that too."

"What's in it for you?"

"The satisfaction of helping a good human being. And whatever you think the information is worth to you. It is negotiable. Here's my personal number you can reach me on," he said, extending his arm with a crumpled note.

"DO NOT ENGAGE, SHUT UP!" I could imagine Viraj whispering in my ear.

"See you next week," I said, closing the cab's door.

On the ride home, it occurred to me that mom had no idea about my wedding or the annulment proceedings. I wondered how she would react if she learned about it. Would she support my restraint? Would she nudge me to be more proactive and avoid repeating the mistakes she made in life? Would she say keep fighting for my marriage or would she advise me to run and protect myself? I called her as soon as I got home.

"Mom, I've been jetlagged and I neglected to call you these past few days."

There was silence for a few seconds. I could hear her breathing.

"I called your US number. The voice on the other end said you had already left for India."

"Why didn't you leave a message with her?"

"I didn't know how to."

"Well, what's wrong? Is grandma all right?"

"She is fine."

"What is wrong then?"

"Are you sitting down?"

"Yes, I am! Out with it!"

"Venkat killed himself."

"What?"

"Yes, exactly on the day you got on the flight to India."

"I'll get the next flight to Star City then!"

"There's no use. The funeral already happened yesterday."

"Do you know why he did it?"

"I think he left a note saying he was disappointed with how nobody understood his love."

"How are Aunt Lakshmi and Uncle Mohan taking it?"

"They're devastated. Folks from his office were at their place and our place."

"Why our place?"

"They wouldn't tell me. They left a number and insisted on talking to you directly."

I hung up and dialed the other number right away.

"Sorry about your cousin. We're all devastated," the lady who picked up the call said. "There's no easy way to say this, but you were the beneficiary listed on his life insurance policy."

"That's impossible. It should've been a girl named Shanti."

"Shanti was the primary beneficiary, but we learned that she killed herself the same day. It seemed like a coordinated move. You were listed as the contingency."

I stared at the blank wall.

"Hello, are you there? It will take us a few days to mail you a check. We will need some basic information from you."

"OK."

"Aren't you curious how much the policy was worth?

"Not really."

"His annual salary. $20,000, give or take."

***

I slept on the news about Venkat. I slept through it. I barely slept.

I combed through the PI's data for the details of the guy blackmailing Bina. I then walked straight to the phone booth.

"Is this Kamal Dutta?" I inquired.

"This is him. Who's asking?"

"I'm a delivery guy holding a package in your name. Did you order a mobile phone? Nokia 7650?"

"That's the latest model but you must have the wrong number."

"I will return it to the sender then."

"Who is the sender?"

"Some post box number out of Gurgaon. Thanks for being honest."

"Listen, it's possible that it's a surprise gift from someone."

"That's possible. Why else would it have your name and phone number? Please don't feel obligated though."

"When do you deliver?"

"My route got disrupted and doesn't go your way until this weekend. If you want to meet me at Sarojini Nagar market, I'm driving past there tomorrow."

"Sounds good. See you there."

The next day, I waited beside Manpreet Apparel, our planned meeting spot. I was holding the phone I purchased in a bright yellow plastic bag that could be seen from a mile away.

"Are you the delivery driver?"

"Yes and no."

"Why are you changing your story now? You must be corrupt."

I handed him prints of the email exchanges between him and Bina. The attachments included the compromising material Kamal was using as leverage.

Kamal's jaw dropped. He fidgeted with the papers.

"Are you a cop?"

"No, just a well-wisher."

"I can't believe Bina had the guts to share this information with someone."

"She didn't. She doesn't even know I'm here talking to you."

"What if I just walked away?"

"You can have this brand-new phone for just listening to what I have to say next."

He grabbed the plastic bag from my hand. "I'm listening."

"Again, you're free to walk away whenever you feel like it. Why did you blackmail Bina? Honest question."

"She broke up with me out of the blue."

"What's wrong with that?"

"I was pretty invested in her. All I wanted was an explanation."

"So, you weren't doing it for the money?"

"Not at all. After all other efforts failed, I just wanted to draw her into a conversation."

"You know how Bina is, right? What do you think the odds are she will change her mind?"

"Very low."

"What if I gave you the money you're asking for to disappear from her life for good?"

"How do you know I will keep my word?"

"How do you know I won't go to the cops with the blackmail evidence I have? I don't have all day; do we have a deal?"

"Yes."

"Enjoy the phone. Don't use it to record people without their consent," I said, as I walked out of the market.

***

"There is new energy on their side, as if a burden has lifted," Viraj noted over the phone.

Silence here was intentional.

"Are you there?" Viraj asked.

"I'm here, just thinking about next steps."

"Meeting two is almost here, have you thought about what you're going to say or do?"

"Can I play it by ear?"

"Yes, you can. If you can live with the outcome."

"What do I have to lose?"

"You mean other than a wife and the thousands of dollars you've spent so far?"

"Oh yeah, I didn't think about that."

***

As we walked in for the second mediated meeting, the assistant extended his hand, as if attempting to shake my hand.

"It's good to see you too," I said, ignoring the hand.

"Same rules as before," he said, opening the conference room door.

Something was different about the room this time. It could have been lighting. Or furniture. Or the carpet pattern. I couldn't tell.

As Mira sat down, her shoulders seemed more relaxed than before. There was no preamble from Rajesh or Viraj. Just silence.

"How is your mom doing?" I inquired.

Mira looked puzzled but collected herself.

"She is a fighter. They are doing chemo along with the Whipple procedure. It will buy her time but doesn't guarantee anything."

"I'm sorry to hear how much of a weight it is on you all."

"It is a part of our life now. How is your mom holding up?"

"She is her robotic self, nonstop and reflexive action. Now that dad is gone, there is no one to put a damper on it."

"It must be tough on her, living by herself and taking care of grandma."

"That it is. How is Bina doing?"

"She was going through a bit of a rough patch, but things seem to have let up for now."

"I'm happy for her."

"Are you?"

"I know she is a pragmatic person who has made it her mission to protect you. She deserves happiness too."

Mira's puzzled look re-appeared.

"How is the money situation?" I asked. "I'm sure the Delhi move, sending two kids to graduate school, and so on must have taken their toll."

"It's tight, but I think we will make it."

"Because we're still husband and wife, I wanted to share something for your consideration."

"What?" Mira said, hiding a smile.

"A family member passed away, and I inherited some insurance money. I think using it for your mom's treatment would honor their memory."

She scanned my eyes with hers.

"You know I can't take you up on that offer."

"No rush. The offer is open, just holler if you change your mind."

"We have ten minutes left," Mira said, glancing at the clock on the wall.

"I think we have more than that."

A smile and a pause.

"Give me one example of how I could have made you feel emotionally safer using a past situation," I inquired.

"I wasn't expecting that question but let me think."

"Take your time."

"You can say no to me without worrying about consequences," she replied.

"When exactly?" I probed.

"Whenever it is relevant. No upper limit on the number of times."

"I want to understand more about that," I suggested.

"And that's how the cookie crumbled!" Rajesh said, already gathering his papers.

"Good work guys, you made good progress today," Viraj observed, setting his empty glass down.

I saw Mira get into a car with Bina and an elderly gentleman I presumed was her father. I wished I could talk to him man to man, Viraj permitting.

I didn't know how long I walked after stepping out. I paused at an autorickshaw stand. When the autorickshaw guy dropped me off at Piyush's apartment, I tipped him a dollar bill. He held it up and admired it.

***

"The suspense is killing me guys!" I confessed.

"What do you mean?" Piyush feigned surprise.

"You and Aditi under one roof," I clarified.

"We're trying to understand it too," Aditi replied, before Piyush could say anything.

"Just like that? No plans or expectations?"

"For now, yes."

"Lucky bastards. What I wouldn't give to be in your position."

"Grass is always greener on the other side," Piyush dodged.

"You haven't had one argument since I got here!" I countered.

"That's true. How about I make some mocktails to celebrate your progress and our being together?"

"Sounds great! And I owe you an explanation about Priya!"

"I'm all ears," Piyush said, mixing drinks at the kitchen counter. "Aditi, Priya was the girl KK pursued during his younger years in India."

"I ran into her at a bank in Scottsdale. She told me my idealism threw her for a loop, and she was too indecisive to make a call."

"How did that work out for her?"

"Not very well but I wonder if my then intensity would have smothered her, and if she saw right through it."

"Life does not let you model simultaneous what-if scenarios, unfortunately," Piyush offered.

"True. And it boggles my mind to think that if Piyush wasn't beaten up, I would never have met Mira."

"Where is my thank you?"

Everyone chuckled.

"In our parents' generation, divorce or annulment was unthinkable," I said.

"I think we're overcorrecting now," Aditi chimed in.

"How do you mean?" I asked, sipping on the who knows what.

"We follow our parents' patterns and expect different results. And head for the exit prematurely instead of problem-solving."

"We need a psychology test for becoming a spouse or a parent. Strictly informative and non-binding obviously," I declared.

"That is something I can drink to," Piyush said, raising his glass.

"Can you spike my drink? It's not doing anything."

***

I kept revisiting the scene where the car receiving Mira did not have her mother in it.

I looked up the hospital details in the PI files. I hailed a cab.

"Are you family?" the receptionist asked.

"More of a friend, may become family in the future," I responded.

"You're not listed as a visitor in the system."

"I must get back to America shortly and I may never get a chance to see her again. But I wouldn't want you to violate any hospital policies for me."

"Can you make it a quick in and out?"

"I sure can."

I was guided to the exact room. I walked through the door and approached the bed cautiously.

Mira's mom lay there unconscious and frail. Sensors and equipment seemed like natural extensions of her body.

"Is this how she is most of the time?"

"Morphine has that effect," the nurse responded.

"Can I touch her hand?"

"You can but you need to wash your hands first. Risk of infections is very high."

I complied.

When I touched her, I thought of the meeting when Mira and I held hands and didn't realize an hour passed by.

"Thanks for giving me Mira," I whispered.

She shifted, as if to acknowledge my gratitude.

"How much longer does she have?"

"I'm not at liberty to discuss the details."

"I understand. I'm sorry, I didn't mean to pry."

I turned around to leave, and Bina entered the room. She stopped in her tracks when she saw me.

"How did you know where mom was?"

"Isn't what I'm doing here a more important question?"

"Yes, and so is how you got in here."

"Mira mentioned some dark clouds lifted for you recently. I'm happy for you."

"I can't for the life of me imagine how you visited from a different country knowing everything that has happened to our family."

"Can we step out into the waiting area? I want to honor your mom's need for some rest here," I offered.

"I want mom to know. We're not keeping secrets from her."

"I know Mira and you share a soul, but I want to know where Mira ends and you begin."

"What do you mean?" Bina asked, folding her arms.

"Does Mira get an equal say in your day-to-day life? Does anybody else for that matter?"

"DO NOT ENGAGE, SHUT UP!" Viraj's voice in my head tried and failed.

"Nobody gets to walk into our lives and take my sister away from us."

"Did it ever occur to you that Mira chose me?"

"She didn't think it through!"

"She planned an entire trip around a surprise wedding. And it was the best day of our lives. She is an adult who knows what is good for her."

"To me, both of you look confused in that photograph. Did you see your expressions?"

"Say it was the biggest mistake ever. I have a question for you."

"Damn right it was. Get it over with!"

"Every time you encounter an issue, big or small, who solves it for you?"

"I do."

"Then let me and Mira do the same thing. I don't know whose

problem you are solving by trying to fix our lives!"

"Who are you?" Bina scoffed.

"Your brother-in-law."

"I wish I had spared my mother from this argument."

"Well, I hope she heard everything."

CHAPTER 12: HOLDING THE CENTER

"Can you believe this is our last mediated meeting?" I asked.

"All good things must come to an end," Mira replied.

"Cruel play of words!" I said, running my fingers through my hair.

There was a long pause. Rajesh and Viraj seemed intrigued.

"You're the more evolved one between the two of us. I'm growing but I may never reach my full potential. Even if I got there, it may never become visible to you from a distance. I thrive on exhaustion but I'm worried that I will pull you down with me. The only logical next step is for me to give you what you're asking for," I said.

"Can we end this meeting and save us all some time?" Rajesh interjected.

"Not so quick," Viraj replied.

"Before we close the loop, I have a few questions," Mira said, flipping a notepad open.

"OK," I said, wondering where this was going.

"If the Piyush attack incident were to happen today, what would you do?"

"Call an ambulance."

"If your boss expected you to work late consistently and that got in the way of your personal life, what would you do?"

"Ask for overtime compensation or resign."

"If you met a beautiful girl outside a pharmacy today, what would you do?"

"I'd tell her I'm married."

"OK, that was a trick question."

"If someone told you that you had to be better educated and look better to qualify for a relationship, what would you do?"

"Convey that my self-worth was not negotiable. Take it or leave it."

"If someone grazed your girlfriend in a crowded market, what would you do?"

"Report the incident to the cops. Move to safety."

"If someone asked you about a girl you pursued in college, how would you react?"

"Admit we were not a good fit. Not get blackout drunk to evade an explanation."

"If your body told you, you were exhausted, what would you do?"

"Get adequate rest."

"If you were visited by a corrupt assessor, what would you do?"

"Decline to pay a bribe."

"If you saw a black marketeer physically and verbally assaulting a woman in public, what would you do?"

"Call the police. Step away."

"If I were to ask you to marry me in 30 minutes, how would you respond?"

"I would marry you but not today."

"If a petty thief ran out of the store with an item, what would you do?"

"I would not agree to help the friend in the first place!"

"KK?" Mira nudged.

"OK, stick to the store policy and not chase the guy out the door."

"Congratulations, we are graduating to a trial," Mira said, closing the notepad.

I looked at the clock. We were 13 minutes over.

***

There were 10 days before we went to trial. I booked my first domestic flight in India, from Delhi to Star City. Grandma had slowed down considerably. The burden of running the house alone was beginning to show in mom's wrinkles and gray hair.

"Mom, we need to get you help."

"What do you mean?"

"Hire someone who can do chores around the house and bathe grandma."

"Reliable folks are hard to find around here."

"Do you have time to go shopping later today?"

"Sure, we need to get you some new clothing. You wear the same stuff all the time."

"Let's do that," I said, not mentioning there was jewelry shopping on the agenda too. "I wish dad was around to go with us. I can't believe it has already been six months."

"After you left for the US, they found two blockages in his arteries. He wouldn't let us tell you about it. So, don't blame yourself too much," mom cautioned.

"He was done with this world long before his time came," grandma noted.

"Venkat's life insurance policy benefitting you has become quite the discussion in our extended family," mom said, serving tamarind rice for lunch.

"I'm not surprised."

"In fact, Aunt Lakshmi and Uncle Mohan plan to ask you for all of that money to be passed on to them."

"When will we learn to treat grownups like grownups, mom? I wouldn't have helped Venkat if it wasn't for Aunt Lakshmi's request in the first place. Do they not see the irony in that?" I wondered aloud.

"Mom, you need to get a passport and then apply for a visa so you can come visit me in the US," I added.

"Who is going to look after your grandma while I'm gone?" she asked.

"Aunt Lakshmi?"

"As you may have noticed, they instantaneously combust when they are under the same roof."

Three days into the Star City visit, the phone rang.

"Mom, can you pick up the phone?" I said, feeling too lazy to get up from the couch.

"You do it. I'm doing laundry in the backyard," mom yelled from a distance.

"Hello, this is KK."

"Hi, it's Mira."

I switched the TV off using the remote.

"Hi wifey, what's going on?"

"How is the preparation for the trial going?"

"I've been ignoring emails and questions from Viraj. By answering this call, I'm also ignoring his advice about engaging only through him."

"You're a lousy customer to have."

"And a lousy husband, I'm told."

"So, I have some news."

"Yeah?"

"Mom is conscious."

"That's awesome news!"

"She heard you question Bina."

"Oh no," I said. "Please convey my apologies if we disturbed her peace."

"She's siding with you."

The remote slipped from my hand.

"That is encouraging, but I'm convinced Bina will not back off."

"Well, there is some news in that department too."

"Which is?"

"Bina learned that you put some sense into Kamal Dutta's head."

"That was supposed to be a well-guarded secret."

"Thank goodness it wasn't. Here I am, wondering when you became so meticulous with strategy."

"You haven't even seen the trial yet," I blurted.

"About that, we are withdrawing the annulment petition."

Was this how a sudden onset of weightlessness felt like?

"Whose call was it?"

This was the longest pause in our phone call history thus far.

"We need to consummate the marriage before any of this changes again," I said, attempting to move past the awkwardness.

"When Mira came to visit you in the hospital, we were all very impressed with her. How serious are you about Mira? People approach us with potential matches for you, but I put them off saying you're still studying," Mom said, as I set the receiver down.

"Let's talk about it when we go shopping. You should help me pick some clothes for her too," I replied, hiding a smile.

Waking up the next morning was hard, but I wanted to believe the guy who said everyone who sets an alarm to wake up in the morning was an optimist.

ABOUT THE AUTHOR

V. R. Koti lives in the suburbs of Atlanta, GA, with his wife, son and daughter. He runs his own green building consulting firm, and collaborates with owners, architects, and engineers. When he is not working, he enjoys writing, photography, physical activity, and spending time with his family.

Koti's professional work in systems and sustainability deeply informs how he observes people, institutions, and power. His work draws from real experiences of migration, love, loss, and adaptation across cultures.

Author will monitor reader feedback on www.theragingmigrant.com
Please consider posting your review on Amazon and Goodreads.